DEDICATION

To those who still read to children, and enrich them with
our traditions. With thanks to Freddy Grice, whose little
tome of 1944 inspired this one.

Table of Contents

Table of Contents

Dickie of Kingswood

There was once a very clever thief named Dickie who lived off his wits near Kingswood in Allendale. One day, he was travelling home after a long spell in the south. He was weary and hungry and stopped to rest a while by a cottage at the side of the road. The woman who lived in the cottage had been widowed a year before and had recently married a wealthy farmer who treated her badly and frequently told her she was stupid. Dickie overheard them talking.

"Woman," the farmer said in a cruel voice. "Do not light a fire today. I am hiding this bag of gold up the chimney." She agreed she would not, and the farmer stuffed the bag up the chimney. Then he went out to the stable, saddled his horse and rode off down the road. He passed Dickie on the way but his mind was too full of other things to notice him.

Dickie waited until the farmer had disappeared and then went to the cottage and knocked on the door.

"Who are you?" asked the woman.

"Why, I'm Dickie of Kingswood!" he said brightly.

"Where do you come from?"

"Paradise," he joked.

"Oh, my," said the woman, suddenly brightening, "Maybe you have news of my poor dead husband?"

"Indeed I do," said Dickie, quick to take advantage. "He cobbles shoes in heaven and eats nothing but cold cabbage leaves."

"Goodness," said the woman. "Had he no message for me then?"

"Yes," said Dickie, thinking he might be able to get a few shillings out of the woman. "He asked if you could spare him a little money as things are a bit tight for him at the moment."

The foolish woman fell for it completely. She rushed over to the chimney and returned not with a few shillings, but the whole bag of gold. Dickie needed no second bidding. He took the bag and made off with it leaving the poor witless woman in her garden thinking she had done something grand for her dead husband.

You may imagine the scene that took place when her farmer husband came home.

"I cannot imagine anyone doing anything so stupid!" he bellowed at her. "You have to be the most stupid person in the whole world!" And with that he went back out and mounted his horse and galloped northward to try to catch up with Dickie and the bag of gold.

The farmer had not ridden but an hour when he came upon a strange sight: there, lying in the middle of the road on his back, was Dickie of Kingswood. The farmer got down from his horse and asked what was happening, which was exactly what Dickie had hoped for. He had heard the approach of the horse and correctly guessed it was the farmer. So he had dropped to the ground and was shading his eyes against the bright sun.

"It's a miracle!" said Dickie. "What a fantastic sight!"

"What is it?" asked the curious farmer.

"I see a man flying away," said Dickie. "Come, look for yourself!" And the farmer lay down on the ground and cupped his hands over his eyes.

"Where is it?" he asked.

"Open your hands and you'll soon see a man flying away from you!" cried Dickie, and with that he leapt onto the horse and rode off laughing loudly. The farmer stood up and, as his horse and the bag of gold disappeared over the horizon, he was left with the thought that perhaps there was maybe one person in the world more stupid than his wife.

As Dickie rode toward Kingswood, he decided to sell the horse, so he stopped at a farmhouse and was given a good price for it. As he walked off, he noticed two fine bulls in a field. They were beautiful animals and Dickie decided to steal them. As soon as he was certain no one was around, he climbed over the wall and led the animals out of the field and cushed them along the road. He knew people would recognise them, so he decided that he had better head towards Carlisle to sell them at market. All day he drove them along the narrow roads over the Pennines and towards the west.

At dusk, he was still a long way from Carlisle, and fearing the farmer would catch him, he turned the bulls into a nearby paddock. He was about to abandon them, but suddenly someone called out to him.

"My! Those are the best pair of bulls I've seen in many a year." Dickie looked around and saw a tall man riding a beautiful black stallion.

"They are fine animals, sir," Dickie said. "I'm on the way to Carlisle to sell them at market. If you were to save me the trouble I could let you have them at a very good price." And the tall man looked them over and agreed to buy.

"It's dark almost," he said. "Come stay the night at my house and you can be on your way tomorrow. Dickie took him up on his offer and the two men sat down to a large supper, then settled before the flickering fire to talk over a tankard of beer.

"That's a fine horse you have," said Dickie. "Are you not scared someone will steal it?"

"Not at all," said the tall man. "I am an inventor and I have devised the most cunning lock to keep thieves out of my stable." Then, because he liked Dickie so much and had got the bulls for such a reasonable price, he invited

Dickie to take a look at the lock while he explained how it worked. Well, of course, the next morning came and the horse and Dickie and the money from the bulls were all gone!

As Dickie rode back to Kingswood in style and comfort, he saw a short man coming along the road who was puffing and blowing and looked very tired.

"All right mate?" Dickie said.

"Not really," said the poor fellow. "Someone stole my prize bulls and I've been told he's on the way to Carlisle to sell them. I'm just about worn out and I don't think I can go any farther!"

Again, Dickie was quick off the mark.

"I saw those bulls!" he cried. "You'll need to hurry though, they're in a paddock not two hours away!"

"Would you sell me your horse?" asked the short man, and Dickie said yes, of course, and sold the horse to the man from whom he'd stolen the bulls. When he got back to Kingswood he put together all the money he had made and bought himself a nice little house. And sometimes he sat on the porch and smiled and wondered what must have happened when the tall man and the short man met each other on the Carlisle road.

The Humshaugh Ploughman

When air was clean and waters pure, there lived in the Northlands all manner of faerie folk, some good and some evil. Something they all shared, however, was a distrust of humans, and they made every effort to keep themselves out of sight. Nowadays, they have either perfected the art, or have gone altogether. Whichever is true, they are, for the most part, remembered with fondness, like this one.

The early morning mists had blown away to reveal the ploughman already hard at work behind his team of Shire horses. He toiled in the fine spring morning near the village of Humshaugh, a beautiful place close by the river of the North Tyne. As he progressed the seagulls and corbies swooped down on the unearthed worms in the furrows behind him and the air filled with their shrill cries. In the May trees, thrushes and blackbirds were singing at the top of their lungs, while the occasional feathery-poke threaded in and out of the hawthorn hedgerows. The bees buzzed busily between the lamb's tails as they danced in the breeze and the ploughman was very content in his work.

As he passed under the catkins he could hear the steady grinding of the faeries as they churned their butter. He did not stop his work though, for he had heard the sound many times and he knew that no good would come of his interference. So he turned his team around and cut the sod in the opposite direction. When he returned at the completion of the furrow, however, the churning has ceased and he heard a small piping voice cry:

"Alas and alack! I've broken my staff!"

"Leave it for me on the oak stump and I'll fix it," he said with a smile, but he did not wait around, instead he turned the horses again and ploughed another furrow in the field. Sure enough, when he returned, there upon the stump was a tiny broken churn staff. He took out his knife and cut a piece of willow twig from a tree and fashioned an entirely new staff from it, and, placing it on the stump, he again turned to his work. On his next return, he saw there on the very spot where he had left the new churner, a pat of shining yellow butter, his reward for being such a very kind ploughman.

Fitzheugh of Cotherstone

Teesdale, historic boundary between County Durham and the North Riding, was once covered in dense, beautiful woodland. High in the dale was the castle of Cotherstone with its peaceful village gathered around its walls. It was the home of the Fitzheugh family, and every now and again huntsmen gathered there before going after deer in the Lune forest nearby. The young Lord Fitzheugh, last of his family line, was very keen on hunting and often led parties into the forest.

One day, when the dawn came bright and clear and the sky seemed to stretch forever, he announced there would be a hunt. The autumn air was crisp and cold at first, but after a while it mellowed into a fine day. The baying of the hounds filled the air as he hoisted himself onto the broad back of his chestnut hunter. Fitzheugh blew on his horn and turned the horse to cross the cobbled courtyard into the narrow lane that led to the village. Suddenly, a woman appeared in his path. She held out a cane and stopped him, then said with fear in her eyes,

"My lord, you must not go hunting today. There is grave danger. Turn around and go home!" He looked down on her with a puzzled frown.

"What danger?" he asked. "I see no reason to stay away from the hunt, stand aside and let me pass." But the woman was adamant.

"I must warn you sir, do not go near the Percymyre Crag, there is danger there."

"Well, I'm aware of that!" said Fitzheugh for he had heard of unwary travellers who had become lost in the fog on the moors and had fallen from the crag to their death.

"Today I have cast your fortune," went on the woman. "And it has shown great misfortune at that place!"

"Very well," said Fitzheugh, anxious to be rid of the woman. "I promise I will not go near the Percymyre Crag. But I shall go hunting."

He saw a look of relief come into her eyes and, smiling at her, he rode on. Something about the woman disturbed him however, because she had not asked for payment, as fortune-tellers usually did. Still, hunting was his passion, and he was determined to go.

Turning the corner onto the village green he met with his favourite sight — horses and hounds, and after a tankard or two of ale, the hunt set off in pursuit of deer. Though they had set out in blithe spirits, the huntsmen were soon frustrated. When the dogs picked up the scent, the hunt would charge off at full speed only to find out after hours of wasted chase that they had been on the trail of a fox, or else the scent would lead into a beck and be lost. The weather too was not kind. It had taken a sudden turn for the worse and black clouds began to roll in over the moors to darken the land even further.

Just as the fog rolled in and the rain began to fall, Fitzheugh realised he had become separated from his friends and although he called out several times, he could discern no reply. He decided then that he had better make his way back to wait for the others in the warmth of the castle. He whistled his dogs, which had stayed close by him, and began to pick his way from the moors back into the forest. Soon the rain stopped and the mist gave way to a more pleasant afternoon and he felt a little more cheerful.

Suddenly, across a clearing in the trees, a large and handsome hart stepped from the shadows and looked directly at Fitzheugh. Immediately the young lord pulled his horse about and, sounding his horn, charged off after the deer. The hounds barked and bayed, and the horse snorted as they raced through the bracken and over fallen trees. Hard and long went the chase. Now Fitzheugh could see the deer, now it was lost. The frantic chase covered many miles, but Fitzheugh was engrossed in the chase and did not notice the distance he had covered. The hunter and the hunted became tired — the dog's tongues hung out and they ran more slowly, and the horse was covered in a white foam of sweat, but the deer was running for its life and on it went. And Fitzheugh would not consider giving up the chase.

The shadows grew long and the light became dim and the young lord had no idea where he was. But just as he thought he might just be catching the deer at last, the Percymyre Crag opened up before him. Too late, he pulled hard on the reins. But the Fitzheugh line ended right there as the hart, hounds, horse and the young lord plummetted over the edge of the cliff.

The little priest of Felton
The little priest of Felton
He caught a mouse
Within his house
And no one there to help him!

The Middridge Faeries

The little village of Middridge lies between Newton Aycliffe and Shildon in County Durham. There's an old quarry there, very near what is known locally as 'the faerie glen.'

Long ago, when summers seemed longer and warmer, there was a boy at Middridge who was prone to boasting. Everybody knows someone like this, they are called Clever Dick, or Smart Alec, or, like the boy from Middridge, Know-it-all Jack. It didn't matter what the subject was, the chances were he'd done it, seen it or been there.

One day, some of the boys from the village were busy gathering and eating brambles from the hedgerows and they talked of the faeries that lived in the quarry and underground round and about. Most agreed that they were not friendly and remembered the warnings they got from parents and grandparents about leaving them well alone. Jack, as usual, knew different. He said that the whole story was just a pack of lies told to the little one to frighten them and keep them away from the quarry.

"Anyone who believes that is stupid!" he said. He always said that at the end of a statement because it meant that anyone who disagreed with him would not feel like saying so in case the others thought they really were stupid. This time, however, one of the boys was so fed up with Jack and his wild boasts that he spoke up.

"Just how do you know that?" he asked.

"Why, because nobody that I know of has ever seen a faerie," replied Jack.

"But that's because nobody was ever brave enough to ride around the quarry nine times," said the other boy. "And no one ever will, because if they do, the faeries will come above ground and deal with them!" Jack still insisted that the faeries did not exist and called the other boy stupid. When asked if he would dare ride around the quarry, he laughed and said of course he would but he did not own a horse. Jack stopped laughing, however, when the other boy offered the loan of his father's horse.

"You could ride round the quarry right now," he said. "It's Sunday and the men are not working." All the boys looked at Jack and he realised that he had backed himself into a corner with his boasting. If he refused to accept the challenge he would look cowardly in front of his friends. So he reluctantly accepted and told the other boy to borrow the horse. Then they arranged to meet back at the stable an hour later.

By the end of the hour all the boys had returned. Jack looked very confident, and he mounted in a cheerful mood.

"Well," he said, "We'll see now if there are faeries in the quarry!" And off he went amid the cheers of his pals who were only too happy it was not any of them who was to prove or disprove the old stories. They stayed right where they were, at the stable a good way across the fields.

Now, Jack was a boastful boy but he was also quite bright. During the hour it took to get the horse, he had talked to his grandmother and asked what he should do if he were ever chased by faeries. She told him that no faerie could pass by rowan bark without stopping to pick it up. So he went immediately to a rowan tree he knew and stuffed his pockets with bark. He felt he would be safe either way, and went off to prove the tales wrong.

When he arrived at the edge of the great pit, however, his courage waned just a little and as he peered into the depths below he began to wish he was safely back home. He walked the horse slowly all the way around the edge of the quarry. After the first circuit, he stopped to listen, but he heard nothing and had more confidence. As he progressed, he rode faster and faster until after the ninth time and he still could hear nothing, he called out:

> "Ye faeries, ye faeries
> Wi' yer iron gads,
> Dare not fight
> Us Middridge lads!"

But even before his laughter had stopped echoing, a spine-chilling cry came from the quarry.

"If your horse is not well-hayed and fed,
I'll catch you up and see you dead!"

The blood drained from Jack's face and he stayed only long enough to hear something scurry up the quarry face and not a second longer. He spurred the horse and rode as he never had before, head down and back straight. But in no time he heard a scuffling right behind him. Thinking quickly, he threw a handful of rowan bark flakes into the breeze and the faerie stopped dead in its tracks. Jack kept riding as fast as he could and it was just as well, for just as he arrived at the stable and crashed down from the horse, the faerie released a spear. It missed only by a hand's width and gauged a large hole in the doorpost by the cowering boys.

You may be sure that none of them taunted the faeries and, if you ever go to Middridge, maybe one of the village folk will show you the mark in the doorpost that the faerie spear made.

King Arthur's Cave

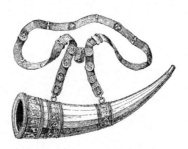

An old shepherd sat down on a great rock high on a hill above the Roman wall in Northumberland. It was midday, late in the spring, and all the sheep had lain down in the heather to rest. As the bees buzzed in the sunshine, the shepherd rolled wool as he kept an eye on his flock. Far below, in the ruins of Sewingshiels castle, a yellowhammer sang his bright song.

As the shepherd sat daydreaming, a raven flying overhead croaked loudly. The shepherd looked up, shading his eyes with one hand, and as he did the ball of wool fell from his other hand and tumbled into the heather and down the steep hill. The old man looked over the edge of the rock.

"Well," he said, "At least it fell in a fairly straight line and should be easy to rewind." Then he picked his way through the heather and whin down the side of the hill as he rolled up the yarn. Suddenly the trail of wool disappeared into a hole in the ground. The shepherd pulled away the undergrowth and stared into the darkness.

"Bless me," he said, "It looks like a cave or something." He pulled away the heather and found the entrance was quite big enough for him to climb in. Then he eased his way into the dark cave and was surprised to find that he could stand up with room to spare. When his eyes grew accustomed to the dim light, he saw a long passageway before him. At the far end there seemed to be a light. The shepherd felt compelled to investigate. He cautiously approached the light and soon the passage opened out into a large room where the light seemed even brighter. But what was in the room made his eyes open wide in disbelief. There, beneath an ornate stone archway, was a company of soldiers dressed in ancient battle garb and seated around a great table. They seemed to be asleep. Each was wearing gauntlets and holding a sword, and their metal helmets gleamed in the eerie light. Right at the centre of these men was one soldier taller and more striking than the others. To the shepherd, this man's older features seemed to show great kindness and wisdom.

"This is just like the story I heard when I was a lad," thought the shepherd. "This is King Arthur and his knights — fast asleep waiting for the call to come back and rule England!" He sat down on a ledge and tried to remember the old tale of Arthur and how he didn't die but was taken by his men to a place where they all slipped into a dream waiting to be roused when needed. He remembered the rhyme his teacher had taught:

> "Draw the sword, the garter cut
> And sound the bugle horn;
> Then Arthur once again shall reign
> O'er England he has sworn."

The shepherd looked again at the table, and there indeed was a hunting horn, a garter and the fabled sword, Excalibur. He approached the company and boldly took up the sword. It was a great deal heavier than he had expected, and it glinted in the cold light. He slipped the garter along the blade and quickly severed it. All that remained was to blow the horn, but as he reached for it, the king and his men began to stir—yawning and rubbing their eyes. The shepherd's courage failed him, and he turned and took to his heels. across the cave and down the passage to where he had first entered the cave. As he scrambled up toward the daylight, he heard a voice, deep and full:

> "O, woe betide the wasted day
> This witless wight was born!
> Who drew the sword, and cut the cord
> But never blew the horn!"

The shepherd had no intention of stopping, either to find out who was speaking or to offer a reply. He just kept on climbing until he was at last lying panting on the heather above. After a while, his courage returned.

"I have been a fool," he thought. "That was Arthur, the greatest ruler we ever had. I'm sure he would have brought peace and prosperity." And he began back down the hill, intending top go back into the cave and blow the horn. But he could not find a trace of the opening—not a fern nor shrub was bent out of place. He came back again and again over the years, but he had forever lost the chance to sound the awake to Arthur and the Knights of the Round Table.

Leg's Cross Hill and Bildershaw
Mak' many a hoss to puff n' blaw

The Lorbottle Cuckoo

Three farmers sat outside the village inn at Lorbottle in Northumberland. They drank ale from pewter tankards and talked about their work. Mostly, they discussed the possibility of rain coming to spoil the upcoming harvest, and how much better it would be if the dry days of summer could stretch just a little further into the autumn to make life a little easier.

"You know," said one of them. "I've noticed how the weather changes as soon as the cuckoo arrives. The spring rains stop and the whole place warms up."

"You're right," said one of his companions. "And as soon as she leaves again, the weather turns for the worse!" There were nods of agreement and more ale was ordered. Then a thoughtful look came over the face of the third farmer and he leaned forward with an expectant expression on his face.

"If the cuckoo brings the warm weather," he said. 'And then takes it with her when she leaves, it stands to reason that if we could think of a way to keep the cuckoo here longer our problems would be solved." The other farmers thought for a minute and agreed heartily, wondering why they had not thought of it sooner.

"How shall we make the cuckoo stay, though?" said the first farmer. Again, the men fell into a silence, rubbing their chins and scratching their heads. The second farmer spoke up.

"What if we catches her an' keeps her in a cage?"

"That'd do fine," said the third farmer. "But I'm too old to go chasing around after birds, they're mighty fast you know." And the men stopped again to think.

"We'll take her by cunning!" said the first farmer. "We'll wait till it's night time and she's fast asleep, then we'll creep up to the rosebush where she roosts and pin her in with wicker walls!" Now this seemed the ideal plan. They drank more ale and proceeded to figure out the means whereby they could capture the cuckoo and keep the summer at Lorbottle.

Over the next few days the men worked on building three wicker hurdles, wide enough so that when put together end to edge they would completely surround the rose bush. When the moon rose on the third night and the men were sure the cuckoo would be asleep, they crept across the fields from three different directions towards the rose bush. Gently, they placed the edged of the hurdles together and pinned them securely. Then, stepping back to admire their handiwork, they gave a great cheer. And the bird hopped up and over the hurdles, and with a final 'cuckoo!' flew off into the night.

"The cuckoo comes of mid-March
And cucks of mid-April
Then gans away of midsummer month
When the corn begins to fill"

The Cauld Lad of Hylton

Long ago, at Hylton Hall, near Sunderland, there lived a small, lively and mischievous brownie whom the servants called the 'Cauld Lad', because he wore no clothes and Hylton Hall was a cold kind of place in those days. This little fellow had a habit of  turning the day's work upside down after everyone had gone to bed. The chairs and tables would be thrown on their backs and sides, and the dishes would be taken from the cupboards and strewn about the kitchen along with most of the cutlery. Food would be taken from the pantry and liberally spread around the place (especially the flour, for the Cauld Lad liked nothing better than to see clouds of this white powder cascading through the air.) If the ashes from the fireplace were still warm, he liked to rake them out, spread them over the hearth mat and lay down on them .

But sometimes, just when the scullery maids could stand no more of the brownie's pranks, they would come into the kitchen and find the place spic and span, even things that they had left unfinished were tidied up and put in their proper places! So contrary was this faerie that they never knew what to expect next.

One night, near Christmas, the cook and her husband were returning from an evening out, and it was very late, so they entered the hall very quietly so as not to disturb those already asleep. As they crept past the darkened kitchen, they noticed a strange light coming from under the door, and, as they went to check what it was, they heard a small voice, singing:

> Wae's me, wae's me,
> The acorn's not yet
> Fallen from the tree,
> That's to grow the wood,
> That's to make the cradle
> That's to rock the bairn,
> That's to grow to the man
> That's to lay me!

The cook pushed the door until it was slightly ajar, and peered into the kitchen. There, sitting on the edge of the table, and swinging his legs over the side, sat the brownie. He looked a forlorn little thing, wearing such a frown as might suit a child who is tired and refuses to walk any farther. He was about as high as a milking stool, and his skin was brown as you might expect, but it was covered in fine hair, so that he had the warm looks of a rabbit, though he was far too thin to be mistaken for one! His eyes were big as horse-chestnuts and their colour almost the same, and the cook and her husband smiled with delight when they saw his pointed little ears!

But at that moment he heard a tiny noise from them, and he was gone in a flash.

"Where did he go?" asked the astonished cook. Her husband did not know, but they suspected that they had scared the little fellow off, and that he would not return that night, so they took themselves off to bed.

The next day the downstairs parlour was full of talk of the Cauld Lad, for this was the first time that any of the servants had actually seen the brownie. The cook told everybody said what a cute little chap he was, and those who had not seen him were very disappointed indeed. Then the gardener suddenly said :

"You know, when I was a boy my father told me that brownie was under a spell." The others immediately wanted to know more and the gardener went on to tell them that the Cauld Lad had been always been mischievous and had once angered the Faerie king who placed the brownie under a spell which made him stay at Hylton Hall. Although he would much rather be with his own kind, in a place of which men know nothing, he must stay until such a time as someone released him from the spell. That, he told them, was the reason that he caused such a mess about the place, in the hopes that someone would banish him forever.

"Just how would we go about this spell-breaking?" asked cook, who had become most distressed at hearing the story.

"If I remember right," the gardener replied, "He has to be offered a gift of something which is not perishable, and if he accepts it, we'll see him no more."

This made the cook sad to think he would be gone forever, but she decided that it was the best thing to do for the brownie himself. So she set about making him a cloak and a hood, which he would be proud to show off once he reached the land of his own people. All that evening, she toiled away sewing and cutting and stitching until at last she had the finest hooded cloak that it was possible to create. It was of the smoothest silk, and lined with shimmering satin. Her husband told her that it was a wonderful gift that she had made for the Cauld Lad.

Late that night, they laid the cloak upon the kitchen table, and then hid themselves in a root cellar at the far end of the room, where they could watch without being seen. Quietly they waited, as the hall clock ticked away the minutes, and chimed away the hours. At last, the dim light that they had seen before now glowed near the table, and as they strained their eyes to see, they could make out the shape of the Cauld Lad as he went immediately to the place where the cloak lay. He looked at it with the suspicion at first, then, on picking it up and holding it out, he saw that it was his size and must be meant as a present. His eyes lit up and an enormous smile stretched over his face from ear to ear! The cook and her husband were smiling too, but this time they were sure to make no noise in case they were to frighten the brownie away again. Carefully, the little faerie pulled the cloak across his shoulders and tied the draw cord around the neck. How splendid he did look! He skipped around the table-top and sang with delight:

"Here's a cloak, and here's a hood,
The Cauld Lad of Hylton will do no more good!"

And with that, he jumped in the air, snapped his fingers and disappeared ... and has never been seen nor heard from that day to this!

Ovington Edge and Cockfield Fell
Are the coldest spots between Heaven and Hell

The Lang Man o' Bollihope

There was once a giant that lived up on Bollihope Common in County Durham. He was ill tempered, as giants can be, and the folks of Weardale feared him greatly. He never came down off the Common, but whenever he found a man up there he'd kill him without mercy. The dalesmen were afraid to take their sheep up to the moors when he was around, so they did most of their shepherding with border collies running to the whistles and shouts from the lower fields. But the giant liked nothing better than raw mutton, and they lost lots of sheep over the years. Sometimes, when the summer was particularly hot, the giant came down to the river at Frosterley and drank all the water so that there was drought lower down the valley. But he was the biggest thing that ever roamed the Common and the dalesmen could do nothing about it.

One day, another giant came from Cumbria in the west. The news of his arrival spread fast, for giants are very jealous and will not tolerate another of their kind. Everyone hoped the two would fight, for fights between giants are always to the death. The Bollihope giant came back from the edge of Hamsterley Forest where he had been trampling trees for fun. He immediately scented the intruder and the dalesmen ran for cover when they heard his terrible war cries thunder down the valley. The Cumbrian answered with equal ferocity, and the two giants charged toward each other with earth-shaking steps. They uprooted the last two oak trees on Bollihope Common and used them as clubs. Blow for blow they exchanged, from noon to midnight, through the night and into the following day. Both were terribly wounded, but both continued the fight.

The people of Weardale dared not come out of doors to watch, until at long last the shattering sounds stopped and died away like thunder rolling over the Pennines. Then, cautiously out they went. There was no sign of either giant, and they guessed correctly that the Cumbrian had won and they would no longer have to live in fear.

Eagerly they climbed up to the Common to take a closer look at the fallen giant. But when they arrived they found nothing but a huge mound of rubble and rock which to this day is known as 'The Lang Man o' Bollihope.'

Says the River Pont to the River Blyth -
"Where thoo droons one, Aa droon five"
Says the River Blyth to the River Pont -
"Aye - an' the mair shame on't."

Pollard's Lands

The northlands were once carpeted in lush forest; sprawling hardwood giving way to taller conifers where the land rose high above sea level. The woods were filled with grey-eyed wolves, brown bears, wild boars, and other ferocious animals long since extirpated. Wild boars are the ancestors of domestic pigs and once were plentiful in England, and some of them were especially vicious.

One such boar lived in the woods to the west of Bishop Auckland in County Durham. People had reported the animal to the Bishop of Durham who lived in Auckland castle as they were prevented from attending the market because they were afraid the animal might attack them on their way in from Weardale.

So the Bishop posted a reward for anyone who could put an end to the great boar.

Hunting parties occasionally went out, but the boar always seemed to elude them, and very few people were brave enough to tackle it on their own. But one young man decided that he would kill the boar and claim the reward. His name was Pollard.

He went into the wood and climbed a tree to keep watch on the comings and goings of the great animal. Pretty soon, he discovered that the boar like to gorge itself upon beech mast then shuffle its way into the undergrowth to sleep off the meal. Pollard went early one day to one of the boar's favourite beech trees and shinnied up it to the very top. He shook the branches so that lots of beech mast and nuts fell to the forest floor, then he sat back and waited for the boar to come along.

Not long after, he heard the animal grunting in delight below him as it fed hungrily on the feast Pollard had shaken down. And it ate until everything was consumed — then, just as Pollard had predicted, it went off into the ferns and rolled on its side and fell fast asleep.

"This is my opportunity," Pollard said to himself and climbed hastily down the tree. He followed the boar into the undergrowth and crept quietly up to it. He pulled out a sharp knife and plunged it deep into the sleeping boar — but the boar would not die so easily. It leapt up and attacked Pollard so suddenly that he fell back and was gauged before he had time to think. Quickly he rolled to one side, slashing with the knife all the time. The boar attacked again and the young man grappled for his life, cutting and stabbing all the while. The fight went on for almost an hour, then with one last grunt, the great boar fell to its knees and died. Pollard cut out the boar's tongue, then he went to find water, but before he had gone fifty paces, he dropped exhausted into the ferns and fell fast asleep.

A little while later, a merchant was riding along the woodland path on a two-wheeled cart and he chanced upon the boar lying dead by the wayside.

"This is my lucky day," he thought. "The boar has been killed by some other creature and all I have to do is take it to Bishop Auckland and claim the reward!" And with that, he threw a rope around his horse and dragged the dead boar onto his cart, then he set off toward the bishop's palace.

When Pollard awoke, he was dismayed to discover the boar missing. At first he thought perhaps he had not managed to kill it after all and it had run off, but when he saw the fresh marks along the cart track he knew that someone had taken the boar—and he guessed at once where they might be headed. He turned and ran toward the town as fast as he could.

Even as he arrived at the palace, he heard the bishop saying to the merchant,

"You have rid us of a great menace and I shall reward you as promised."

"My Lord!" cried Pollard. "It was I and not this stranger who slew the great boar, and here is my proof!" And with a sweep of his arm he slapped the boar's severed tongue on the floor beside the boar's head.

Seeing this, the merchant admitted he had merely found the dead creature and had not been the one to slay it, so the bishop offered the reward to Pollard.

"I am no less pleased that it was you who put an end to our fears," he said. "This shall be your reward: Take a horse and you may have as much land as you can ride around in the time it takes me to dine this evening." So saying, the bishop and his attendants retired to the dining hall, not in any great hurry, for he was a generous man, and was at dinner a full hour before returning to the great hall. To his surprise, however, Pollard was already there waiting for him.

"You are back so soon," said the bishop.

"I did not ride far, my lord," said Pollard. This pleased the bishop, and he smiled.

"And how far did you ride?"

"Why," said Pollard with a twinkle in his eye, "No farther than around your lordship's own palace." The attendant looked toward the bishop in silence, but to their surprise he just threw back his head and laughed heartily.

"You have not only outwitted the boar, but the Bishop of Durham as well!" he said. Then he laid his arm around

Pollard's shoulder and led him to a window overlooking the Wear valley.

"Though I cannot be true to my word and give you this palace, I can offer you that land there." He pointed to a parcel of land rich in pasture and meadow and asked if Pollard would exchange the two, and the young man said yes. And those lands are to this day known as Pollard's Lands and the whereabouts marked by Pollard's Inn.

In Darnton town there is a stone
And most strange it is to tell
That it urns nine times round about
When it hears the clock strike twelve

The Lambton Worm

Lambton Castle is on the banks of the River Wear not far from Durham. Long ago, John, the young heir to Lambton was fishing in the river for trout. Now this seems a very ordinary thing for a boy to do, but he was doing it on a Sunday, which in those times was deemed a very bad thing.

"Sundays are the Lord's Day," a passer-by said to him. "You should be at church, not here fishing!" But the youngster took no notice and kept right on tying together his fishing line in full view of everyone.

Earlier that day, he had found a wasp's nest and dug it up, sustaining only one sting as he beat a hasty retreat when the yellow-jacketted throng took to the air upon being disturbed. Fifteen minutes later he went back and picked up half a dozen little white grubs to use as bait, for wasp grubs are one of the favourite foods of trout.

Very confidently he walked down to what looked a likely spot and cast the bait into the water. It plopped into an eddy and young Lambton laid the rod in the fork of a stick pushed into the bank and sat down to wait. No sooner had he made himself comfortable than the rod bent and he had a bite! Quick as a wink he jerked the rod and set the hook. The fish took off and almost pulled him into the river,

"This one is a fighter," he said to himself. "It must be a salmon or a sea-trout!" Then the two of them battled on for a while until at last Lambton managed to haul the fish onto the riverbank.

"What kind of fish is this?" he said aloud, holding the creature up by the line and hook. "This is the ugliest thing on earth!" What Lambton had caught was thin like an eel, but it also had legs, two at the front and two at the back, much like a lizard. Whatever it was, he had no intention of touching it, and looked around to see how he might get it off the hook without using his hands.

A little way off in a neighbouring field there was a well with a trough nearby that cattle used to drink from when the river was in spate. Lambton ran over to this rod, line, worm and all. He dangled the creature over the well then, putting his boot against it, gave a mighty tug and the worm fell down into the black water below. Lambton returned to the river and kept on fishing until he had a brace of trout to take home. And he though no more about the worm.

Years later, Lambton went to his father and announced his intention to go overseas to fight in a foreign war.

"This is no life for me, Father," he said. "I should be in battle, testing my skills as a soldier." And although the father had no desire to see his son leave, he gave his blessing and wished him safe. Over the months following the departure of young Lambton, the estate grew to be a sadder place, for although he had been a rake, he was missed much. Then, in the second year after he was gone, strange things began to happen around the castle. Shepherds began to find dead sheep around the place — few to begin with, but soon it became one every night, half eaten and left in the pastures. The milk yield from the cows dropped so drastically that before long the castle had to send to Chester-le-Street for enough to get by. The lord of the castle set men to keep watch through the night and they discovered that a great ugly worm that slithered each evening from the well by the river caused the mayhem. It was the self-same creature that young Lambton had thrown there all those years previously. And what a change ... it was enormous and fearful!

Many of the servants tried to kill it, but it always got the better of them. Each time a piece was hacked from it, the worm slithered over it until it reattached itself. After it had been attacked, it would roam the countryside in a grievous mood and do more damage than usual, uprooting trees and smashing down fences, so that after a while, people gave up trying to kill it. The old lord decided instead to try and keep the worm from getting angry by pouring many churns of milk into the trough by the well, and by tethering two sheep there each night. So the worm grew even bigger and the people grew even poorer. The land around the castle became quite barren and nobody ventured out at night to watch the worm slither from its lair in the river to wrap itself three times around a nearby hill before going for the food left out for it. To this day, that place is known as 'Worm Hill.'

One day, there came into the castle yard a single charger upon which was mounted a knight, Tall and handsome, clad in shining armour and wearing a smile on his bronzed face. At once he was recognised as the young lord, back from his adventures in foreign lands, safe home from the dangers of war. A celebration was ordered at once and that night the great hall was filled with all the folks from around about.

During the feasting, young Lambton leaned over to his father.

"What has happened to all the trees on the south side of the castle? Has there been war here?" His father looked sad for the first time that evening, and as a hush came over the gathering, he told the tale of what had transpired during the son's absence. By the end of the story, a darkness had covered the young man's face.

"It's my fault this worm destroys our land," he said solemnly. "It was I who first imprisoned it in the well and so it must be I who must rid Lambton of this wicked menace." And with this, a cheer went up from the crowd at the renewed hope brought by this new champion.

The next day, true to his word, young Lambton began to ask questions in order to put together a plan to get rid of the worm. He listened closely to the stories of the worm's remarkable healing powers, and he learned its habits and its wants. Then he went to visit a witch who lived near Durham.

"You must await the worm at his island in the river, and attack while it is still in the water," she told him. "You must stud your armour with sharp spikes and razor-edged knives, and you must show no fear."

"That sounds easy enough," said Lambton. "What do I owe you for this information?"

"I need no reward," the witch whispered softly. "But the spell itself requires that you kill the first living thing you meet after slaying the worm. Otherwise, for the next nine generations no Lambton will die peacefully in his bed."

So when the young man got back to the castle, he told everyone what the witch had said, and instructed his father to let loose one of the dogs as soon as the hunting horn was blown to signal the death of the worm.

The following day Lambton settled himself among the rocks and ferns on the island in the river and awaited the arrival of the great worm. Presently he saw its fearsome outline against the riverbank as it entered the water, and he slid into the water and waded towards it. The worm seemed to recognise him instantly. In its fury it lashed its tail, sending sheets of water into the air. Lambton set about the serpent with his sword, slashing and cutting. This time, however, when a piece was hacked off, it drifted away in the river before it could be reattached. When the worm wrapped itself around Lambton it cut itself terribly on the spikes and razor-edges, and the more it tried to crush him the worse it sliced itself to pieces. Desperately it tried to get back to the riverbank, but Lambton kept hacking away until it closed its fiery eyes and was swept away dead down the river. The young man crawled exhausted from the water and blew a shrill note of victory on his hunting horn.

But when his father heard the sound, he forgot that he was to release the dog, and instead set off himself to check on his son. To Lambton's dismay, the first creature that he met after slaying the worm was not his hound as he had expected, but his own father and of course, he could not kill him. So what the witch foretold came to pass, and for nine generations following the death of the worm, no Lord of Lambton was to die peaceably in his bed.

The Blind Man and the Statue

In the market place at Durham is a statue of Charles Stewart, Lord Lieutenant of County Durham. When the statue was first made and put on display, it was the talk of the city, and people came to the marketplace especially to see it. Everyone that saw it said it was the best statue they'd ever seen and soon the sculptor became quite proud about his work. In the evenings he would join the men outside the market tavern and openly boast.

"This statue is the finest in England. It's perfect! There is not a single fault to be found with it. It is a masterpiece worthy of any city in the world!"

The self-praising sculptor would invite people to test it for faults, but they could find none. This made him more intolerable than ever. So much so that everyone was trying to spot some little imperfection on the carving just to shut him up! One of the servants of the Lord Lieutenant himself came and examined the statue, hoping that the face or body of the rider was in some way wrong. They were not. A horse dealer from the town of Appleby came to look over the horse. He thought to find fault with the anatomy of the beast, he checked its muscles and its mane, fetlocks and hind quarters, even the veins to see if they were out of position, but they were not. A saddler came to look over the leatherwork. It was correct. A tailor came from Leeds, a specialist in military uniforms, hoping that the tunic was missing a button or a piece of braid, but it was not. The creation was as if it had been alive and turned to stone.

After a time, no one bothered to look at the statue, as it seemed useless to search for a fault. This did not prevent the sculptor from bragging, however, and day after day he infuriated the townsmen with his boasting.

One day, there came tap-tapping of a stick, as a blind beggar picked his way along the walls toward the tavern. When he got to where the men were sitting at the outdoor tables he said aloud:

"Would you kind gentlemen care to hoist me up onto the statue?"

The men looked at him briefly then burst out laughing.

"Do you meant examine it?" asked one of them.

"Why yes," replied the blind man. "For although I do not have my eyes, I am amply compensated by the sharpness of my other senses."

The men were only too pleased to oblige. They lifted him onto the statue and sat back to watch as he groped his way over every curve and contour of the sculpture. At noon they offered him a tankard of ale, but he refused and carried on with his examination. At three in the afternoon they offered again, but he said no, and kept up his search. The men went home for their evening meal at about six o'clock and it looked as though the beggar would do no better than everyone else. Surprisingly, he was still at it when they returned around seven o'clock.

"What does he hope to find?" some asked. "All of us with good lamps could find nothing. The beggar is a fool!"

As the blind man's fingers moved down toward the carved horse's head and around its nostrils and mouth, it appeared that the sculptor's claim of perfection would be endorsed once again. The beggar finished his inspection and asked to be lifted back down from the monument. and again the men obliged.

"Who carved this statue?" he asked once safely down on the ground.

"I did," said the sculptor stepping out of the shadows, proud as a peacock.

"It is a fine piece of work," said the blind man. "Probably the best statue in the realm." The sculptor beamed and looked around the disappointed faces outside the tavern.

"Except for the mistake ..." said the beggar. A hush fell over the gathering and all eyes were directed toward the statue.

"That horse," said the beggar slowly, "Has no tongue."

The men gasped aloud and almost tripped over each other in their haste to validate the claim. Two of them climbed up and a few seconds later cried:

"It's true! The horse has no tongue!"

A rousing cheer went up from the men and they picked up the blind man and carried him into the tavern to reward him with a celebration for his having, at long last, found what the rest of them could not. The sculptor, however, was overcome with the news. He disappeared into the evening and feeling he could never face the men again, he took his own life.

Later the same night, the blind man slipped quietly away and was never seen in Durham again.

When Roseberry Topping wears a hat
Morden Carrs will suffer for that

The Ji-jaller Bag

In the days before the steam engine, and the times before the coal mines cut scars across the North Country, there were pretty villages scattered all around the outskirts of Newcastle.

In one of these villages, long long ago, there lived an old hag who was a thief and had robbed the villagers for years. No one could prove that she was responsible for the thefts, but they were fairly sure. In the end, the woman grew too old to rob her neighbours and stopped her thieving way of life. Often, as she felt she could no longer manage herself, she would hire a housemaid to do her cleaning and dusting for her. It was always one of the village girls and they were always paid out of the money that had been stolen.

Each time she hired a girl, before they started work, she would tell them, "Clean everywhere except the chimney. If you poke about up there all the soot will fall and we'll have a fine mess to be sure!"

Usually the girls did just as they were instructed, leaving the chimney alone and cleaning everywhere else. One girl, however, wondered why the woman had bothered to mention this in the first place, for housemaids did not clean chimneys anyway as the sweep was always called in to do that job. She suspected that the stolen money must be hidden there!

That evening, as she was about to finish and go home, the girl noticed that the woman was fast asleep in her favourite chair so she crept across the kitchen to the fireplace and poked the end of her broom up into the dark flue. Down dropped a bag! The girl did not stop to look inside, but quickly turned toward the door and ran outside leaving the old woman still sleeping in her chair.

As the girl ran along the way, she came to a gate. To her surprise the gate spoke and said to her:

"Pretty maid, oh pretty maid
Open me I pray,
For I've not been open
For many a long day!"

The girl looked at the gate and then over her shoulder for the old woman, and said,

"Open yourself gate, I have no time." Then she turned and kept on going. Soon she met a cow standing to one side of the path, and the cow too spoke to the girl:

> "Pretty maid, oh pretty maid
> Milk me I pray,
> For I've not been milked
> For many a long day!"

The girl looked at the cow and then over her shoulder for the old woman, and said,

"Milk yourself cow, I have no time." Then she turned and kept on going. Soon she came to a mill, and the mill too spoke to the girl:

> "Pretty maid, oh pretty maid
> Turn me I pray,
> For I've not been turned
> For many a long day!"

The girl looked at the mill and then over her shoulder for the old woman, and said,

"Turn yourself mill, I have no time." Then she turned and kept on going. Meanwhile the old woman had woken up to find a pile of soot on the floor of the kitchen and her money gone.

"My ji-jaller bag! My wee leather bag!" she cried. Then she hurried after the girl. Soon she came to the gate.

"Gate o' mine, gate so fine,
Have you seen that girl o' mine
Wi' a ji-jaller bag
And a wee leather bag
Wi' all the money in it
That I ever had?"

And the gate said "Farther on ... " The old woman walked along until she met the cow.

"Cow o' mine, cow so fine,
Have you seen that girl o' mine
Wi' a ji-jaller bag
And a wee leather bag
Wi' all the money in it
That I ever had?"

And the cow said "Farther on ... " The old woman walked along until she met the mill.

"Mill o' mine, mill so fine,
Have you seen that girl o' mine
Wi' a ji-jaller bag
And a wee leather bag
Wi' all the money in it
That I ever had?"

And the mill said "In the hopper!" So the old woman walked around the back of the mill, opened the hopper and found the girl and beat her soundly. The very next day she hired a new girl to do the housework, and once again told her not to clean the chimney. Well, the new girl had already heard that the last housemaid found the stolen money up the chimney, so as soon as the old woman fell asleep she took the bag down and ran off with it. This time when the girl came to the gate, she opened it. When she came to the cow, she milked it, and when she came to the mill, she turned it. Then she ran off down the hill to the village. When the old woman woke up she set off after the girl, but when she asked her gate if it had seen the girl, the gate said nothing. When she asked the cow if it had seen the girl, the cow said nothing. And when she asked the mill if it had seen the girl, the mill said nothing. So the girl escaped with the money and the people of the village shared it out.

The Brown Man o' the Moors

On night, a traveller was crossing the Simonside Hills on his way to Rothbury in Northumberland. The hills have a bleak beauty, but are dangerous when fog comes in or after nightfall. Crags and deep ravines, so obvious in daylight, become dark and fill with mist and shadow, blending in with the hills themselves and disappearing into the background. The outcrops of rock become slippery and treacherous, and the traveller was distressed to realise he was lost.

The young man had judged the distance he needed to walk and had set off early in the day, but he did not know that there were few features on the hills to guide him. Where there were no trees or buildings, and a long uninterrupted horizon, he soon wandered far off the right track and round in circles. The shepherds who worked on the hills knew the whinny bushes and the streams that led downhill and to villages, but the traveller did not. When the last fingers of sunlight slipped behind the Cheviots he wrapped his coat close about him, braced himself against the cold, damp air and prepared to spend the night on the bleak hillside.

As he clambered around in the dark, he came upon a large rock and sat down on the leeward side with his back firmly against it. He began to whistle, then he remembered that this is supposed to attract the devil, so he stopped. A few minutes passed and, as he began to fall asleep, he noticed a little way off the silhouette of a hut or cabin against the gloomy night clouds. From it came a dim light. At first he thought it must be a fire fly or will o' the wisp, but he brightened up in the hope that it was a fire. He got up and went toward the hut on his hands and knees, fearful that he might fall into a ravine in the dark. He moved around the hut to the door, which was slightly open.

"Hello!" he cried, but no answer came and he peered warily around the door to find the room deserted. There was a fine fire in the middle of the room, though, and the traveller lost no in inviting himself in for a warm. Two large stones were either side of the burning embers and upon one of these he sat and began to enjoy the warmth of the flames as they danced merrily about his cold feet.

The traveller was overjoyed to have found the hut, for he knew he would have surely perished left exposed to the bitter cold night air. He looked around. All that was in the hut was the two stones, some kindling by the fire, and two logs — as long as his legs and as thick as his arms. Suddenly the door was crashed open and in stepped a small brown man with a scowl on his face. The traveller knew at once that this was one of the Brown Men o' the Moors. His coat was of worn lambskin, parchment coloured and ragged. His trousers were of black moleskin and his shoes were brown and threaded with silver. He took off a moss-green cap from under his hood and tossed it into a corner as he sat down on the other stone and scowled at the traveller. The young man was frightened, but he knew better than to enter into a conversation with a faerie, so he just stared back in silence. The Brown Men o' the Moors held humans in great contempt and flew into rages at the slightest provocation. They never went near the dwellings of men and had never been on friendly terms, and the traveller knew the little man was not to be trusted.

As they held each other's glare without blinking, the fire in the centre of the room burned slowly down to embers and the night began to touch the traveller once again. He pulled his clothes closer about himself, then leaned to his left and grasped a handful of sticks and twigs and dropped them onto the fire. He folded his arms, drew his knees up to his chest and kept an eye on the Brown Man who sat statue-still.

Suddenly, the Brown Man picked up one of the large logs, though it was a big as himself, and smashed it over his knee as if it had been matchwood. He threw it into the fire, giving the traveller a challenging look as if to say 'can you not do better than a wee Brown Man?' But the young man was either no fool or else his courage had deserted him. In any case, he remained stock-still for the rest of the night.

As the darkness turned slowly to light, the cold and damp again began to caress the traveller. He was tired and hungry and could no longer keep his gaze fixed on the Brown Man who looked as fresh as when he had first entered the hut. But the dawn came, and somewhere down in the valley a cock crowed and dogs began to bark. Startled, the young man opened his eyes wide, but to his amazement the Brown Man had vanished, along with the hut, into thin air. As the clouds scurried away from the east and the watery sun shone pale on the Simonside Hills, the traveller looked around to find himself perched on the topmost crag of one of the highest hills. To his left was a sheer precipice down to the valley far, far below. Had he taken up the challenge of the wicked Brown Man, he would have leaned out too far to reach the second log and fallen down the cliff to his death.

The Golden Arm

There was once a man who had travelled the entire kingdom in search of a wife but was unsuccessful and at last returned to his home near Gainford. There, he met a young girl who was fair natured and pretty, but it was also of great interest to him that she had one arm made of pure gold. At once he proposed to marry her and she, thinking he loved her for herself alone, said yes.

They were wed almost straight away in the parish church and lived quite happily in a little house near the river. Some years after, there came to the village a disease that took all the weak and sick to their rest, and the girl, though still young, was quite a delicate thing, and she too succumbed to the fever. She was buried in the churchyard and the husband put on a show of grief for the others to see so that they would think him genuinely bereaved. Secretly, though, he was already making plans to return later that night to recover the dead woman's golden arm.

On the stroke of midnight he crept into the cemetery and dug up his wife's body and hacked the arm from it. Then he filled in the grave and left as quietly as he had come.

When he was safely home again, and tucked up in his bed sound asleep, there came the soft sound of foot falls on the stairs which woke him up. He could feel a cold draught on his back and, feeling very scared, he slowly rolled over to see what was awaiting him. There in the darkened doorway stood the ghostly figure of his dead wife. Then he spoke:

"What have you done with your red-rosy cheeks?"
"All withered and wasted away ..."
"What have you done with your lovely red lips?"
"All withered and wasted away ..."
"What have you done with your golden hair?"
"All withered and wasted away ..."
"What have you done with your golden arm?"
She approached, pointing and shouted:
"YOU'VE GOT IT!"

The Fish and the Ring

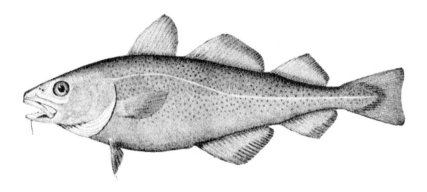

There was once a very learned baron who lived in the North Riding. He was extremely well versed in those things which delve into the mysteries of life and the fortunes of men. He was famous for casting horoscopes and whenever there was a ball held at his castle, the guests delighted to see him perform. He studied a great deal and was not often wrong.

"What is in the stars is your fate," He would say. "You may as well meet it head on, for no one can change fate." He made this announcement each time partly to impress the gathering but also because he really did believe it.

One day, his young son put down his playthings and went to his father.

"What shall I be when I grow up?" he asked. The baron was very pleased and proud that his son should ask. He swept up the little boy and carried him to an armchair. Then he sat down and placed his son on his knee. A great book lay upon the table by the chair, and the baron opened it near the middle. He pointed out various signs and symbols and went on to tell the boy some of the things which would come to pass over the years. Suddenly, the baron put the boy down from his knee and told him to play outside. A shadow passed over his face and he looked again at the open page.

Among the scribblings in the fortune book, the baron had read that one day his son would marry a poor ragged girl who had just been born just a few days earlier in a dirty house near the great Minster in the city of York. The baron pulled his wits about him and ordered a horse to be saddled and brought to the door. As soon as it was ready, he mounted it and rode off to York at the full gallop. A while later, he pulled up the lathered horse in front of the western bar. There on the front step of an old house was a man singing to a crying infant. The man looked very sad.

"What's the matter, my good man?" asked the baron. The man doffed his woollen cap and, lowering his eyes, said, "If it please you sir, my wife and I have five children already, and now this little lass has come along. I couldn't feed the others without going hungry myself, and now I don't know what I'll do." He wept softly and held the new baby closer. The baron was pleased when he heard these words. He raised an eyebrow and smiled at the poor man.

"I may be able to help," he said. "There is a goodly couple at my estate who are themselves childless and I have long been on the lookout for a child they could adopt. If you were to give me this girl, I'm sure they would be very happy to have her and give her a much better life than you could." The poor man was delighted at the prospect and, after speaking with his wife, they kissed the little lass goodbye and handed her over to the baron.

The baron turned his horse and rode off again away from the city. When he was well out of sight, he checked to make sure no one was watching him, then he flung the poor little girl into the river Ouse.

"That's an end to that," he said without feeling, and he trotted off back to his own castle. Now, as luck would have it, the baby was well swaddled and the air trapped in her shawl was enough to keep her afloat for some time. Long enough for her to be spotted by a fisherman who sat on the riverbank mending his nets. He saw the bundle floating slowly past in the current and managed to hook one end of it with a bilge pole that stood by his front door. When he got the baby ashore he was very angry.

"What kind of monster would do such a thing to a helpless child!" he said aloud. Then he hurried indoors to his wife and she dried off the lass and wrapped her warmly in a blanket. From that day, they raised her as their own daughter.

Now it happened many years later that the baron was out hunting deer in the woods near the Ouse. He stopped at the fisherman's hut to beg a drink of water, which the girl—grown up and very beautiful—fetched out to him. The rest of the men in the hunting party teased the girl and embarrassed her by saying how pretty she was, but the baron of course did not know who she was. One of the men stepped forward.

"Let's have her horoscope then! Let's see who shall be lucky enough to marry this pretty young thing!" The baron said that he had no doubt she would end up with a fisherman, but nevertheless he asked her on which day she had been born.

"I don't know sir," she replied. "I was picked out of the river one day by my father some fifteen years ago." At once the baron knew who she was and his face went ghostly white. He made up a horoscope to tell the other men, then he went to the hut. A few minutes later he returned and said:

"Here girl. Take this letter to my brother in Scarborough and it will make your fortune." Then he mounted his horse and the party rode off. The girl was very excited to know that her fortune was to be made simply by delivering the letter and she told her parents about it and a little time later set off to walk to Scarborough.

Now it was quite late in the day and the girl found she had been too eager to set off as the sun began to set before she was half way there. She was scared to continue in the dark so she stopped at an inn and sought a room for the night. Just as she was falling asleep, there was a great commotion downstairs and the girl heard a pistol shot. Then a loud, coarse voice called out for everyone to be downstairs in the next two minutes. They were being robbed! Highwaymen had forced their way into the inn and were stealing everything they could lay their hands on. They searched the girl but found nothing except the letter, which the leader opened without delay. To his surprise, this is what he read:

Brother: Take this girl and put her to death at once.

Well, the robber looked at the girl and saw that she was just as poor as he and that whomever had written the letter must be truly wicked. So he took up a quill and altered the letter to read:

Brother: Take this girl and marry her to my son at once.

So, of course, when the girl finally arrived in Scarborough the baron's brother had the two young people married without delay, and very happy they both were! As soon as the baron found out, however, he made his way to the town and took the girl for a walk along the cliffs. His intention was to push her over, but she guessed it and begged him not to kill her.

"I don't know what I have done to make you hate me so, sir, but if you spare my life I will do anything you ask." So the baron relented, and told her that she must go away and never try to see his son again, and she swore she would. Then to bind her oath, he took a gold ring from his finger and cast it as far as he could off the cliff into the cold sea.

"You may return when you have recovered that ring!" he said. The he turned his back and walked to his brother's castle without a backward glance. The young girl was in tears, for by this time she had fallen deeply in love with the baron's son. She walked slowly away from the cliff, and from Scarborough.

After a while she found a job in the kitchen of another castle near Hartlepool. There she became a wonderful cook, and everyone who ate her food said it was the best they had ever tasted. A year and a day after she last saw them, she heard the baron and his son were to visit the castle where she worked, and she decided to make them the best meal she had ever created. She took up a sharp knife and ran it through the enormous cod that lay on the scullery table and, as she cleaned it out she was both surprised and delighted to find the very ring that the baron had thrown from the cliff! She hid it in her pocket and proceeded to cook the best fish dish any had ever eaten. It was the custom then to call out the cook whenever the dish was exceptionally good. And the fish had been so wonderful that the guests were on their feet and applauding. But when the baron and his company saw the girl, they were speechless. The baron glared and was about to remind her of her promise, when she stepped up to the table and dropped the ring right before him.

"I believe this belongs to you, sir," she said. The baron then realised that what he had said all those years was true: he could not change fate. He stood up and took her hand.

"This is my son's true wife," he said. "And if she will consent to come home with us, I will try my best to make up for all my wrong doing." And he baron kept his word. The baron's son took his young wife back to the castle in the North Riding, and they lived a long and happy life together .

Magpie, magpie, flutter and flee
Turn up your tail and good luck to me!

The Rothley Faeries

There was once a boy who lived at Rothley in Northumberland. He was not a nice boy, but sullen and wicked. He had dark circles under his eyes from lack of sleep as he would stay up late despite the scoldings he received from his parents. After school and during weekends and holidays, the boys of Rothley would spend their time playing football, ducks and byut-the-can, while the girls preferred itchy-dabbers and skippy. Not this boy, however, he would be off somewhere alone, ever seeking to destroy something. In the spring he liked to rob bird's nests of their eggs, and if they had hatched, to tip the gollies onto the ground where they would die. He waited by streams in the evenings and hurled stones at the bank voles when they appeared for a swim. Each day he would break a branch from a sapling and pretend it was a sword, and as he rode his imaginary steed through the meadows, he would swipe the heads from the flowers as he passed by. All in his wake lay waste.

One evening in the summer, when the daylight never quite turns to night, the boy was making his way towards a copse where he thought he might find a rabbit or something to which he could be cruel. In the distance he was just able to hear his mother calling his name as it was time to be indoors, but he paid her no heed. He climbed to the top of a disused kiln and gazed about from this vantage point. The old mill nearby was one of his favourite haunts as he often saw squirrels gathering nuts from the trees beside it, and he loved to throw stones at them.

On that evening, however, something happened which was to change the boy forever. As he sat atop the kiln, his eyes searching the ever-lengthening shadows around the mill for any sign of life, he thought he could hear a noise —strange and elusive noise not unlike running water, but more bell-like in quality. The boy crouched and cowered behind the kiln and peered over the top to find out what might be the cause of the sound. To his great surprise, he saw a faerie train approaching, glowing in blue light and shining like a distant galaxy. As they came closer he could see the wonderful creatures in vivid detail. There were horsemen mounted on white steeds no bigger than a hand, and handmaidens with flowing gold hair and emerald eyes, each carrying a bluebell lantern, which shed soft azure light onto their spangled procession. There were faerie children, small and smiling, and musicians by the score filling the air with their merry and enchanting music.

The whole procession passed inside the kiln through an ash grate near the bottom, and when the last one was safely in, the little portcullis was pulled up and all in the outside world became silent once again. The boy climbed down hardly able to believe what he had just seen. He looked for an opening in the kiln, but could not find one and, as it was getting late, he left for home determined to return the next night.

The following day, the boy could hardly wait for school to finish and fidgeted in his chair so that the teacher had to scold him more than once. As soon as the day was over, he rushed home, wolfed down supper and went up to his bedroom. There, hidden at the back of a drawer, he found the penknife his father had forbidden him to keep. He slipped it into a pocket and ran out of the house and took off in a beeline for the mill. As soon as he arrived he climbed to the top of the kiln and pulled out the knife. He knew that there must once have been a hole at the top where smoke and steam had escaped, but clumps of grass and earth had entirely closed it over the decades of disuse. After a while, he had cleared the hole so that he had a clear view of the inside of the kiln. He could see virtually nothing, even after his eyes became used to the dim light. He called out, but his voice echoed so loudly that it quite startled him and he decided not to do it again. He wanted to drop a stone through the hole to see how deep it was, but he thought the faeries would find it and become suspicious, so he just sat back and chewed a straw.

He had not long to wait. There once again the gentle tinkling sound of tiny bells came over the field and he could see the beautiful lights being carried in procession

to the mill. He crouched down so they would not see him and stayed still until he heard the clank of the metal grate as it snapped shut. The boy knew they were all inside. As he crept sneakily toward the top of the kiln, he noticed a shaft of clear light soaring from the hole up to the heavens, and he was filled with anticipation as he peered into the cavern below.

There, the faeries were celebrating the mid-summer with song and dance and feasting for all. In the centre of the kiln, directly below the boy's face, they had built a fire, and upon it was a pot of boiling porridge. Now and then one of the little creatures would go to the bubbling pot and dip in an acorn cup, take it to one side and eat the contents with a spoon made from a dry straw. Most, however, were too busy dancing to try the porridge.

But instead of enjoying the merriment, the boy was filled with hate for the faeries. He looked around and found a stone in one of the sods he had uprooted. Digging it out, he held it over the hole and carefully lined it up with the boiling black pot below. Then he let it drop. Hot, burning porridge splattered in every direction and the little creatures screamed and wept as they held their hands over their poor faces. The boy was delighted and laughed aloud, but as soon as they heard his wicked voice, all became silent and a hundred little pairs of eyes looked up at him, and a hundred accusing fingers pointed at him. The faeries began to chant, "Burnt and scalded! Burnt and scalded!"

The boy, a coward at heart, ran off, but as soon as he did the faeries sped after him and one of them dealt him a blow in the back with a staff he carried. It was not a hard blow, but the boy fell whimpering into the grass and dared not look up for some time. When at last he opened his eyes, the faeries had disappeared, and they have never been seen at Rothley since. When the boy stood up, he found he could no longer walk straight and, although he never harmed a helpless creature again, he walked with a limp for the rest of his life.

Childe Wynd and the Loathsome Worm

A widowed king once lived at Bamburgh Castle in Northumberland with his daughter Margret. She was a beautiful young woman and had come to be regarded as the lady of the castle since her mother died. In addition to her beauty, Margret was known for her pleasant disposition and great kindness and endeared herself to all she met. Margret had a brother, Childe Wynd, but he had been oversees seeking adventure and fortune for many years.

One day, while the king was travelling in the south, he met a woman and fell in love. Like Margret, she too was a great beauty. She had raven hair and dark eyes, was bright and witty, and made the king very happy when she talked. So the king married the woman and took her back to Bamburgh as his new queen.

As they rode into the town amid great pomp and ceremony, with banners and bunting flying on every house, the new queen waved at the people cheering along the path. She had a streak of vanity, and delighted in hearing the comments on her beauty. The king was very proud, for he was to have the two most beautiful women in the land in his castle.

The king's servants lined the path to the castle, and as the couple arrived at the gates Margret stepped forward to greet them.

"Welcome to Bamburgh," she said in a sweet voice. She hugged her father and kissed her stepmother respectfully on the cheek.

"Well met!" said the king. "Margret, this is your new mother and this is my daughter—isn't she beautiful?"

Beautiful indeed! The queen had never seen such a fair face and was quite taken aback for she had never before had to contend with another for the title of most beautiful. A pang of jealousy ran through the queen as she greeted the princess. Margret did not perceive it, however, for she was as pure inside as she was fair outside. The queen was not sure she cared for this predicament at all, but later she heard something that made up her mind.

As she had not seen the full extent of the castle, a servant was conducting her through some of its rooms, while the king organised the removal of tables in the great hall so that a ball could be held. The queen dismissed the servant and said she preferred to explore on her own. After a few minutes, she slipped unnoticed back into the great hall and began to eavesdrop on some of the people who stood around. What she heard enraged her, for the topic under discussion was the comparative beauty of the two women, and the consensus was that Margret was the lovelier of the two. Then and there she determined to get rid of the young woman and, though to everyone she appeared to dote on Margret, the queen was harbouring an evil plot on that very first night.

For a while, the queen was content in making her new home to her liking. She familiarised herself with all of Bamburgh's nooks and crannies. She had her own quarters separate from all others so she might have privacy to carry on her evil doings. Unknown to the king, she was well versed in the black arts and had performed dark deeds on many occasions. The poor princess Margret, who trusted everyone, especially her new stepmother, had no idea what was going on and when she fell ill from the poisons put in her food, she gladly accepted the queen as her nurse. The queen gave her even more of the evil potions she had made and, one night, while Margret slept, she whispered the incantations of a spell and turned the young woman into an ugly serpent.

"I weird ye be a laidly worm
And borrowed shall ye never be
Until Childe Wynd the king's own son
Come to the Heugh and thrice kisses thee;
Until the world comes to an end
Borrowed shall ye never be!"

The following morning when the maidservants entered the princess' chamber, they saw the great worm and ran out screaming. Princess Margret did not understand, but when she looked into the looking glass, she was horrified to see the serpent's face return her gaze. Slowly it dawned on her that the new queen was a black witch and had done this to her out of jealousy. The tears streamed from the green eyes and dripped from her scaly skin.

Just then the guards rushed in and, thinking the Loathsome Worm had killed and eaten Margret, pricked it with their spears and beat and cut it so that to reach safety it slithered out of the window into the cold morning mists.

The queen was well pleased at the transfiguration, though the king, of course, was heartbroken at the loss of his daughter. From there, he sent to his son, Childe Wynd, informing him of what had happened and ordering him to return home to slay the creature. The worm, meanwhile, took up residence coiled around Spindlestone Heugh, southwest of the great castle. The queen, fearing Childe

Wynd might discover the truth, devised all manner to keep the prince away. She knew only too well that the magic she used would turn against the one who cast it if the spell were to be broken.

The ugly worm grew fatter and more loathsome, eating grass and seaweed and rummaging through the castle middens to feed itself. No one ventured near it, and none had guessed it was poor Margret under her stepmother's spell. On the very day that the king died — broken hearten and not knowing Margret yet lived — word reached Bamburgh that Childe Wynd was returning home to seek out the truth of the tragedies that had befallen his family. When his ship was sighted out on the horizon of the cold North Sea, the queen conjured up a storm that drove the vessel back out from the shore. Huge waves smashed against the wooden ship and the sails were ripped to shreds in the violent wind. The skipper gave the order to come about and move away from the land.

"There is something strange here," he said to Childe Wynd. "The sky is still as blue as blue, and the trees along the shoreline show not a sign of wind, yet we are driven so harshly!"

"There is black witchcraft here," replied the prince. "We must seek another place to land and return later with the ship decked out with rowan branches." So they set off to seek another town further down the coast where they took on board the rowan branches to ward off the effects of witchcraft, then set sail again to Bamburgh. This time, the queen's evil had no effect and the ship went cutting through the waters to the beach. As a last resort, the queen quickly cast another spell over the pathetic worm and commanded it to halt to approach of the prince. The ugly serpent slithered into the sea and thrashed about, snorting and hissing so ferociously that the sailors refused to go on. But the skipper said,

"If we are quick, we can land at Budle Bay before this creature has time to get there!" So they tacked their way north and entered the bay. There was no sign of the worm and before long Childe Wynd stood on the beach, sword in hand and eager to find the loathsome worm that he thought had caused so much sorrow and hardship. As he ran toward the castle the worm crawled out of the sea and reared up before him,. Thoughts of his little sister ran through his mind and he began toward determined to kill the beast and avenge his family.

To his surprise and disbelief, when he reached the worm it spoke! Not in a harsh tone as one might expect, but in a gentle voice. Cowering before him with eyes uplifted, the serpent submitted to the warrior and said:

> "Oh quit thy sword, unbend thy bow
> And give me kisses three!
> If I'm not won ere set of sun
> Won I ne'er shall be!"

Such was the great pity in the creature's soft eyes that the prince was compelled to kiss the worm's huge cracked lips once, twice, three times. There was a shuddering and ripping and the skin fell away from the loathsome worm and there before him was his sister Margret. The two embraced and laughed and cried as Childe Wynd was told the true story of events at Bamburgh.

"Come, Margret," he said. "We must see this wicked stepmother we have and discover why she has cause to hate us so." And he took his sister's hand and led her to the castle. Hundreds of people had gathered and cheered the couple as they reached the gates. Once inside the castle, they went to the queen's private chamber. When she saw Margret, the wicked queen dropped her hairbrush and stared, for she thought the loathsome worm would have been slain and she would have the satisfaction of knowing that Childe Wynd had killed his own sister. As the truth sank in, the evil that the queen had wrought came home to her and, in front of their eyes, she shrivelled and shrank into a warty toad that waddled off into the darkest corner and they never saw it again. Childe Wynd became king at Bamburgh, and he and his sister lived long and happy lives.

They do say, though, that if you are in the vicinity of Spindlestone Heugh, you may hear a low croaking in the grass, and if you search carefully you might find the toad who was once queen at Bamburgh.

The Longwitton Dragon

There are three wells close to Longwitton in Northumberland. These wells have long been highly regarded for the medicinal value of their water. In times gone by, people referred to them as magical wells, and many folks made long journeys to drink the water believing it would heal their sore bones, tired eyes and a hundred other complaints.

One day a farm worker went to the well hoping to take a drink of sweet water to ease his aching back after a long day in the fields. As he arrived, he found a dragon blocking his approach, and as he looked the creature disappeared into thin air. He stood for a moment bewildered, but then he heard a rushing sound and saw the grass before him crushed and bent, and quickly he turned to his heels fearing the invisible dragon was about to devour him. He ran without stopping to the village and spread the news.

The villagers plucked up courage and went to the wells to find out for themselves, and sure enough, they were driven back by the terrible invisible beast. Men returned later still with swords and sharpened sticks and attacked the dragon, meaning to drive it away, but even when they were sure they had cut and pricked it, the dragon seemed to bear no ill effects and grew more and more strong as time went by.

"There's something magical about this dragon," said the farm worker. "It grows stronger every time we attack." And fearing that someone might soon be killed, they decided to abandon the wells and leave the dragon to itself.

One day, a knight rode into Longwitton mounted on the back of a chestnut shire horse and clad as though on his way to wars. He announced that he was in search of adventure, and the villagers were only too pleased to tell him all about the wicked dragon that had cut them off from their supply of magical waters. The knight was keen to take on the dragon and welcomed the chance to show off his prowess as a warrior. The villagers made the knight duly welcome and gave him a hearty supper to build up his strength. He listened carefully as they described the powers of the great beast, and made his plan to meet the dragon at dawn the very next morning. The next day, the knight woke up and, before putting on his armour, took a vial from his saddlebag and liberally rubbed its contents onto his eyelids.

"This potion was given to me by an old woman that lives in the forest," he told the villagers. "She foretold me of this encounter many weeks ago. This lotion will make the dragon visible to me." And with the defence of invisibility gone, the knight would have the advantage.

Amid a great chorus of cheers he climbed up on his horse and rode off. The dragon was still sleeping, coiled around one of the wells, his warty skin glistening in the early morning light and his foul breath hanging in the spring air like frosted clouds. When it heard the approach of the horse, it quickly disappeared from sight. The knight, of course, could still see it, and he rode hard into its side with his sharp lance. The dragon screeched in agony, but the knight attacked again, and again he pierced the dragon's side. The air was filled with shrill cries, so loud that people could hear them far off in the village. They felt sure that this was the end of the dragon and they had already begun to celebrate.

The knight, however, was not so sure. No matter how many times he stuck the dragon, it writhed for a few moments then turned to face him again seeming unharmed. He remembered that the farm worker had told him the dragon seemed to have some way to heal itself, but he thought this had been made up because none of the villagers had been brave enough to get close enough to inflict a wound on the creature. After a while, however, he began to suspect they were telling the truth. So as the day wore on and the knight grew weaker, he decided to retreat back to the village to give the matter more thought.

When he got back to Longwitton, he could see disappointment in the folks who had come out to greet him, for they could see the look on his face and they knew instinctively that the dragon still lived.

"I shall try again tomorrow," said the knight, and he fell into his bed exhausted. He slept soundly for a while, but soon dreams began to disturb him, and he tossed and turned as he thought of the dragon at the wells. When he finally woke, he felt as if he had had no sleep at all. The knight got up and readied himself for what lay ahead, and then mounted his charger and rode off toward the wells.

Unlike the knight, the dragon had slept very well indeed. It was already watching the clearing in the trees for the approach of the horseman, convinced he would return. Soon, the knight arrived, but he did not attack immediately, but rubbed more ointment onto his eyes then just sat astride the horse eyeing the dragon. He wondered how the beast could endure such punishment yet remain unharmed. Suddenly, the dragon lunged at the horse and the knight was taken by surprise and almost thrown. The dragon, strangely enough, did not press home the advantage, and instead backed off toward the well.

"That was odd," thought the knight. "I wonder why he did not come after me then, for I was almost at his mercy." He lowered his spear and rode at the dragon, piercing it once again deep in its side. The dragon roared in pain and lashed out at the horse, but once again it backed off at the last moment and retreated to the well. Then it became clear to the knight ... the dragon was able to heal itself because it had always had its tail dipped into the healing waters of the magical well! That was why it would not stray far.

Once the knight realised this, he dismounted and attacked the dragon with his sword. He fought bravely for a long time and pretended to grow very weary. He stumbled around as if wounded and, sure enough, the dragon was drawn farther and farther from the wells as it tried to finish off the clever knight. At last, when they were quite a way from the waters, the knight ran around the dragon and stood between it and the wells. Too late the beast realised what had happened and, although it fought ferociously, the knight would not allow it to regain the ground it had lost. This time, as it was stabbed and slashed, the dragon's cries were in desperation, for wounded it remained and, at last, fell to the ground dead and disappeared for the last time.

Meg o' Meldon

In the village of Meldon long ago, there lived an old woman who was believed very rich. No one ever saw her spend a penny so they presumed that she must have lots of money stuffed in an old mattress or somewhere. Every rogue in the district had at some time thought about robbing her, for they would all like to have got their hands on such a sum of money, but they all believed her to be a witch and were scared of her. She had a small black cat and this was sign enough for some of them, but in truth she had little money and was happy to let them think she was a witch if it kept thieves away.

One of the men in the village who had long wished to get his hands on the old woman's money, woke early one morning from a dream in which he had seen where Meg hid her money. He dreamt he had seen a well, and at the bottom of it was a leather bag filled with coins! He had also been told that a stranger would meet him on the last stroke of midnight and, provided that he remained silent throughout the entire meeting, the coins would be his.

Well, this troubled the man for some time, for though he dearly wanted to have the coins, he was afraid of the powerful spells which Meg may have put on the money. Some days went by before he finally found the courage to visit the well, which he knew was close by Meldon Tower. He cautiously looked about before peering over the edge, hoping to see the bag. The well was deep and very dark and, try as he might, he could see nothing much at all.

"This is definitely the place I saw in my dream," he said quietly as he scratched his head. "I'll come back here tonight and try to get that money bag out of the well and into my own pocket" With that he turned on his heels and hurried back to Meldon.

As the day wore on, the man became more confident about going back to the well, for he had searched the village and had seen no sigh of Meg. This usually meant that she would be away for some time, though no one knew quite where the old woman went when she disappeared for a few days. As little after it became dark, which was quite late as it was midsummer, he left his house and walked off toward the well. Before long he stood right next to it, and in the distance he was just able to hear a clock strike the twelve strokes of midnight. For some moments he stood in silence and a terrible dread came over him. Should he turn to see if there was indeed a stranger there, or should he simply take flight. He decided to stay and find out. Slowly, he turned his head and looked over his shoulder. There in the gloom of the mist from the warm, damp grass, stood an eerie figure wrapped in a cloak with the hood pulled down and an arm held up so that only the green searching eyes could be seen. From under the wraps came a bony hand that pointed to the well, and the man slowly edged his way toward it. This time when he looked over its lip, he could plainly see the leather bag, faintly glowing in the pail attached to the end of the well rope. Eagerly and greedily he began to haul on the rope. Soon the pail was up and out of the well and resting n the edge of the wall. As he reached in to pull out the bag he cried in delight:

"Aha! Now I have the old goat's money at last!" No sooner had he opened his mouth than the leather purse slipped through his fingers and plummeted to the very bottom of the well. A low laugh at his back made him look around, and there stood the stranger. As the cloak was lowered he saw that it was the old woman, laughing a toothless cackle. But he did not wait to hear anything else. So fast was his departure, that old Meg o' Meldon laughed about it for a long, long time!

Venerable Bede

St. Bede was born in 673 somewhere near Sunderland. When he was seven, he entered the monastery at Monkwearmouth to begin the long years of training leading to the ministry of a monk. Some time later, he moved to the monastery at Jarrow where he spent the rest of his life. During his long tenure at Jarrow he wrote many books, the most famous of which is the 'Ecclesiastical History of the English Nation.'

Despite his great literary accomplishments Bede was careful never to lose touch with the ordinary people, and it was on their account that he made the first translation of the bible into common language, so those who could read would be able to learn for themselves what was in it. For those who could not read, Bede preached the gospels aloud on his travels around and about.

When he grew old, Bede's eyesight grew dim until finally he was completely blind. But blindness hardly slowed him down at all—he kept up his studies by having other monks read to him and dictated when he wanted to write a new book. Nor was he confined to the monastcry, for often he would have one of the younger monks lead him outside where he could feel the breeze on his skin and enjoy the fresh winds as they ruffled his silver hair. Sometimes, Bede would even venture out alone, picking his way along the country paths until he found someone to talk to, or a crowd he could preach to.

One day, on just such a walk alone, he passed by a mischievous boy sitting on a rock by the wayside. The youngster immediately recognised him and decided to play a trick.

"Father," he called. "I have come from some people who wish to hear you preach." The boy suppressed a giggle, for in fact they were at a lonely place with no people for miles around.

"Thank you my son," said Bede. "Would you be kind enough to lead me to them? As you can see, I am blind."

So the boy led him off by the arm hardly able to contain his mirth at the monk's vulnerability.

"Not far now," said the boy. Before long they arrived at a place that was very quiet and the boy thought it an ideal spot to have the gospel preached. He thought it great fun to see the old man stand upon a hillock and stretch out his arms to speak, though there was not a soul between him and the Danish coast, far across the sea.

Bede began his sermon and it was one of the greatest he had ever delivered. His voice became beauty itself, as the silvery words slipped effortlessly from his tongue. The boy had planned to wait until Bede had finished then tell the old man what a fool he had made of himself, preaching to no one, but as Bede reached the end of his sermon, there came the sound of applause and loud voices shouting "Amen, Venerable Bede! Amen, Venerable Bede!" Then the boy realised they were the voices of the trees and the rocks and the very grass upon which the monk stood. And he thought that if the monk's words could move even these things to call out in praise and admiration, then he had been a fool not to listen. The boy went over to where the old man stood and explained what he had done. Bede, of course, forgave him.

When the boy grew up, he often retold the story, always referring to the saint in the same manner as the voices he had heard, and from then on the great monk of Jarrow has been known as the 'Venerable Bede.'

The Dun Cow

Cuthbert, the most celebrated and famous of all the northern saints, was born sometime around the year 634. He spent the early years of his life as a shepherd and was called to the monk's vocation one day as he tended sheep on the hills of Lammermoor. It is said that he saw the vision one day of the soul of Saint Aidan being carried up to heaven by angels, so he decided to leave the fells and become a monk.

Cuthbert travelled widely and was instrumental in establishing Northumbria as the cradle of western Christianity, eventually becoming Bishop of Lindisfarne in 685. Two years later, the devout and devoted bishop died and was buried by his brother monks on Holy Island. Remarkably, Cuthbert's body did not decay, and ten years after his death the monks moved the body from its burial site and placed it in a shrine above ground.

Then came the terror of the Norsemen, who invaded Britain, burning, stealing, killing and destroying. Fearing for the holy remains of their beloved saint, Bishop Eardulf and the monks decided to move away from Lindisfarne and seek a safer place to live. They took the body of St. Cuthbert with them and began a journey which was to last for the next one hundred and eighteen years.

The monks wandered all over the north of England, into Scotland, south into Yorkshire and once, they even set off to cross the sea to Ireland where they knew they would be able to resume their lives in peace. But a great storm blew up very suddenly and they took this as a sign they were not to go to Ireland, and that God wanted Cuthbert's remains to return to his native Northumbria. First they tried one place, then another, until they arrived at Chester-le-Street, where they seemed at last to have found a safe place to settle. They stayed there for many years and it seemed that the Vikings had been repelled forever, but eventually there came an invasion even greater than had occurred in previous years. The monks were again forced to abandon their home and seek a place safe from the wrath of the Norsemen. By this time, Aldhun was bishop and he decided to move south to Ripon.

After the danger had passed, Aldhun decided it was time to move back to Chester-le-Street. But when the monks arrived at a place called Wrdelau, and the cart upon which the saint's body was being carried sank into the soft mud, and the ox pulling it refused to go another step.

"Perhaps this is the sign that we are to go no farther," suggested one of the monks. No matter how hard they tried, the ox refused to move, so they made camp and decided to rest until the next day. During the night, one of the monks had a vivid dream. The next morning he told the others that he had heard a voice telling him to take St. Cuthbert to a place named 'Dunholm.' But neither he nor any of his brothers had heard of such a place. And the ox still refused to move.

A little while later, two women met at the place where the monks had camped. One of them was looking for a cow she had lost.

"Have you seen my dun cow?" she asked her neighbour.

"Yes," said the second woman, "I saw it grazing near Dunholm." And as the woman turned to go for her cow, the ox stood up and followed her. The monks were astounded and eagerly gathered up their belongings and walked with the woman and the ox to the place called Dunholm. There they found a hill almost entirely surrounded by the river, and at the top of the hill the ox sat down by the dun cow. It was there that Aldhun and the monks of Lindisfarne finally built their simple church to house the remains of St. Cuthbert, and it's on that spot that the great cathedral of Durham stands today.

Beware an oak
It draws the stroke
Avoid an ash
It courts the flash
Creep under thorn
It will keep you from harm

The Sacking of Blanchland

There was a time, many years ago, when the English and the Scots warred with each other almost continually. Even when the kings of both nations had signed peace treaties, the people of the Border country would take little or no notice of them, and would continue to make raids across the Cheviots. Many, in fact, made their entire income from these raids, and the bands of Border reivers from England would ride over the border into the south of Scotland and thieve anything that they could haul back home, often killing all who tried to stop them. Just as frequently, the Scots would come pouring out of the night, doing exactly the same thing in northern England, before they too disappeared into the Cheviots on their way back to Scotland.

It was during these times that the monks built a monastery in the hills by the River Derwent to the west of the town of Consett. These monks decided that they would have to build their retreat deep in the woods, safe from the ever-watchful eyes of the Border reivers and their spies. So they did just that, covering the walls with wattle and daub, and painting everything that was outside a drab and inconspicuous colour, and this, along with its location among the trees, made it virtually impossible for any but the monks to find.

The monks lived there peaceably for many years, and the local people came to call the area 'Blanchland', because of the white habit that the monks wore. They lived quietly, and they worked hard, never forgetting that they should not reveal the whereabouts of the monastery. They knew that the reivers would not think twice about robbing the defenceless monks of their golden chalices and fine silver crucifixes.

Well, despite the vigilance of the brothers, eventually the Border reivers heard about the monastery at Blanchland, and gathered up provisions to make a trip into England, so that they might find and sack the riches of the Derwent valley. Word of this raid reached the monks long before the Scotsmen did, however, and the monks took in all the animals, so that they would not make easy targets should the reivers happen upon them. Then they hid themselves away inside the safety of the walls of the monastery, hoping they would not be discovered at all.

It seemed that luck was with them that day, for early in the morning, a thick mist crept up the Derwent valley and hid the whole of the Blanchland monastery as well as all the land thereabouts. Try as they might, the reivers could not discover the monastery, they rode up hill and down dale, searching here and searching there, but no trace of the fabled place could they find. After many hours the thieves, cold, wet, tired and hungry, decided at last that they were not going to find the monastery in the dales, so they turned their horses in the direction of the borderland and set off on the long journey home.

When news of this retreat was learned by several monks who were posted outside the monastery as lookouts, they returned hotfoot to the Abbot with the good news. At this, the head of the monastery ordered the celebrations to begin. The monks laid out a great spread, and invited in all the people from the neighbouring farms to show their joy at the deliverance of the monastery.

The monks had not been the only ones who were hiding from the wrath of the reivers. Many farmers, shepherds and ordinary folk were also hidden away fearing for their own lives, and they were no less overjoyed at the retreat of the reivers than were the monks. So they too turned up at the doors of the monastery and were cordially invited in to join the merry-making. The bell in the church tower rang out the news to the surrounding countryside and echoed back from the distant hills.

This, however, proved to be the downfall of them all. The swirling mist had thickened even more after the departure of the reivers, and they had become hopelessly lost on the hills about Blanchland. So poor was the visibility that day, that the Scots wandered way down into County Durham, and were obliged to dismount and grope their way amongst the stones and rocks of the moors. And it was then that they heard in the distance the peal of a bell.

They realised, of course, that this could be nothing other than the bell at the monastery, and their cursing turned to rejoicing. They thanked their luck for the blanket of fog that had promised to thwart their attempts to find their target, and which had in the end delivered it up to them. Slowly they made their way to the monastery, and with blood-curdling screams they smashed in the doors and laid into the unsuspecting monks with a vengeance. They murdered all within, and after stealing all the sacred objects and whatever else they considered valuable, they put the beautiful monastery of Blanchland to the torch, and burned it to the ground.

The Magic Ointment

The village of Netherwhitton in Northumberland lies quietly five miles or so northwest of Morpeth and at one end of the village there once lived a shepherd whose wife was the local midwife. They had, sadly, no children of their own, but she always took the greatest delight in looking after other people's children. Many times, when someone wished to visit a friend or relative in the next village or town, the midwife would gladly take care of the children while the parents walked there. In those days everyone walked everywhere, as there was no transport, and only a rich man would own a horse. But they did not mind, and the midwife was always happy to oblige.

Sometimes, too, when a woman was ill, and unable to nurse, the shepherd's wife would take in their baby for weeks on end until the mother recovered.

One night, with the cold rain was lashing down outside, the shepherd and his wife were asleep in bed when someone rode up to their door and began to pitch small pebbles at the shuttered window of their cottage. At first, the midwife thought it was just the heavy rain pelting the roof, but at last, she decided that there must be someone outside in need of help. Pulling on her night robe, she lit a candle and crossed the room to the window and, holding it aloft, said softly:

"Who's there?" She leaned her head to one side awaiting an answer, but none came. Carefully she unlatched the shutter and opened it out over. There before the cottage, holding the reins of a hill pony and soaked to his skin, was a stranger in a black hat.

"My wife lies ill," he said "And we've a small boy, I would be indebted if you would come and look at them."

At once the woman closed the window and gently shook her husband, explaining quickly what was afoot and that she was off on an errand of mercy. She wrapped about her a woollen shawl, around her shoulder and over her head, and stepped out into the stormy night. The stranger sat across his pony, and though the woman would have much preferred to walk, he grasped her arm and hauled her onto the back of the pony, and off they sped into the darkness. She could not tell in which direction they were going—nor did she much care, as this was the first time in her whole life that she had been on horseback and she was thinking that it would quite definitely be the last if she should have her way. After a while the pony slackened its pace and the midwife saw, just by the roadside, a small house with a lamp burning in the doorway.

"We are here," said the man as he dismounted. The midwife was so glad to get down from the pony that she was quite unable to hide the smile. Once inside, the stranger turned up the wick in the lamp and hung it high from a roof rafter where it swung for a few seconds before it stopped to shed its soft light around the room. On a bed lay a wife who was obviously sick. In a crib by her side slept the bonniest baby boy the woman had ever seen. Immediately she set about lighting a fire to boil water and replacing the damp bedding with blankets that she had the stranger warm by the hearth. After she had tended the woman, she told the man to keep her in bed for a week or two and to feed her on green vegetables cooked in an iron pot, and boiled cow's milk.

"What of the child?" he said "I have work I must do, and my wife cannot look after him if she is not to leave her bed."

"Well then, if you like I'll be only to pleased to have him with me until your good woman is herself again," she said smiling. The man turned to his wife and they began to whisper to each other. After some time, he stood up and turned to the midwife.

"Very well," he said. "But there is something you must do." He went across to a dark corner and from a cupboard he produced a small pot-jar.

"This is an ointment which must be rubbed on his eye lids every day. You must not forget to do this, not even once." He looked quite stern and so she just said,

"Yes, yes, I shall not forget. I'll do it now, shall I?"

So the midwife sat on a cracket a little way away from the man, who was now sitting on the edge of the bed and talking quietly with his wife. She picked up the baby and looked into his fine blue eyes and then rubbed a smear of the ointment over his eyelids. The baby smiled and she thought that maybe it was a balm to soothe some irritation he had.

"I wonder if it would help my tired old eyes," she wondered, and she daubed her finger into the pot again and smoothed a little on her own eyelid.

At once the room filled with a strange light and when she looked over at the parents they were transformed into a fine king, tall and handsome and his wife a queen, laid on a large down-filled bed, in a fine gown, encrusted with beautiful jewels. Around the room danced small elven creatures, pulling faces and laughing. She realised that they must be a faerie king and queen and this was pixy ointment.

Quickly she removed the look of amusement from her face and began to pack her things to leave for home. The man stood up and helped her to do it and he and his wife thanked her for all her kindness and assistance, and although he offered to give her a ride she said she'd rather walk, as she had the baby and anyhow it had stopped raining, thank you. So the king and queen said their good-byes and gave her a bag of money, ten times more than was usual, but the woman took it and thanked them kindly and hurried out of the door.

"Just follow the path," she heard the king say. Surprisingly she was home after just a few minutes, wondering if she had not dreamt the whole thing, but the baby in the cradle made her sure that it had all been true. She quickly climbed into bed beside her husband, hardly able to wait until she could tell him all about it in the morning.

The next day dawned bright and sunny, and the chorus of bird song awakened the couple from their sleep. Well, the midwife was full of herself as she recounted the happening of the previous night to her awed husband. When she was finished and was rocking the baby in her arm, the shepherd looked at her.

"Wife, this is a fine looking boy indeed! Though I don't think you ought to use the ointment on yourself, I fear no good will come of it. And," he added, "Don't mention this to anyone else either." So his wife promised that she would be as discreet as possible about the baby, and when asked by her neighbours, she told them it was her cousin's child, and that she was looking after him until she returned from visiting a sick friend. This seemed to convince everyone, and none suspected that the boy was a faerie baby, and the shepherd was content to let his wife foster him.

The wife, though, was not as true to her word as she had promised, for every day when she anointed the baby's eyes, she also would put a little of the salve on her own right eye. This meant, of course, that she too could see the mischievous pixies as they scurried amongst the mortals, often creating havoc.

Sometimes a plate would crash to the floor from the table and the owner would take it as being an accident, whereas, in fact, one of the little people had done it on purpose. All of this the woman saw, and when she was asked why she smiled so much at these misdemeanours, she simply said, "Ah! There's more goes on than meets the eye!" and kept on smiling.

One day, in the second week after she had taken in the baby, she had to go to the market in the next village, Longhorsley. Having rubbed her eye that morning with the magic ointment, she could see the pixies about the stalls, and to her surprise, they were stealing cheeses, butter and bread and the like. Now, she felt she must say something, but she knew that only she could see the faeries, and probably nobody would believe her. Perhaps they may even think she was mad, but just then, coming through the crowds, she saw the faerie king in his long cloak and black hat and forgetting about the ointment she waved to him and cried out.

"Good morning, sir! How are you this fine day?" The king came immediately to her.

"You see me today?" he asked.

"Why yes," she replied.

"With which eye do you see me?"

"Why, with this one," she said, pointing to her right eye.

At that the faerie king leaned across the stall and blew in her eye and caused her to have great pain so that she rubbed and rubbed and rubbed. When it finally stopped hurting, she found to her dismay that she could no longer see through it. Fearing the worst she rushed off home to Netherwhitton, only to find that the baby and the ointment had also vanished. And from that day on, she was blind in her right eye.

The Falstone Piper

Miles Robson was famed throughout the North for his ability to play so beautifully on the Northumbrian pipes. He earned his living as a farm labourer, going from stead to stead, doing a job here, then moving on to do another there. In old times there were many such drifters, especially around lambing time, and more still at the shear. All of them were welcome help to the farmer when the day arrived to shear the flock, but none more so than Miles. At the day's end, when all the men retired to the barn after supper, he would play for them on his pipes and bring back the smiles to their work-wearied faces. Each year, he would visit the same farm and at this particular time he was on his way to the shearing at Woodhouses, near Falstone.

Meanwhile, over at the farmhouse, the farmer was engaged in the same old argument with his wife as he ever was. She was one of those people who are blessed with an abundance of energy, and cannot bear to be idle for more than a moment. Even when she stopped her housework to drink a cup of tea, she would be knitting between sips, or carding or sewing or anything to keep her hands occupied. This was a great asset to the farmer, for while he was out on the hills looking for lost or injured sheep, he was assured that the things he could not get around to at the farm would be taken care of by his diligent wife. Besides all the normal chores that a farmer's wife has to tackle, she also managed to turn out butter and cheese and country wines in such profusion that the cottage industry alone was almost enough to earn their living.

However, the farmer was a devout Christian and he insisted that everyone at his farm should observe the Sabbath, and so Sundays were given over to resting and reading and things other than work. He felt that it was one's duty to spend the day with one's family, so that everyone would become close, for he had noticed how families seemed unhappy when the father was only around for a few minutes at a time. So that was his rule, and he made sure everyone kept it, even his wife, though she still knitted, saying it was a pleasure to do so and therefore could not be classified as servile. Well, this led to a few tiffs between the farmer and his wife, because in order for her 'not to do anything' on a Sunday, she would stay up late on the Saturday night and busy herself with the jobs that needed to be done the next day. Often this meant working into the wee hours of the Sabbath, and it was for this that her husband would scold her.

"It is Sunday and you should not be doing housework now!" he'd say.

"The Lord loves a hard worker," she always replied. "He will not mind if I just finish these few things before I go to bed."

The farmer was also concerned that his wife was overdoing things, and he was trying to get her to rest, or at least to slow down a little for her own good. Besides, he too worked hard and he wished to spend Sunday with his wife, and could not do so if she was constantly on the move. So he made a plan to cure his wife's Sabbath breaking once and for all.

The plan meant having to rise even earlier than usual and to make his way over to the neighbouring farm where he hoped he would meet Miles the piper coming in the opposite direction. And so he did. The two men met and shook hands and Miles was more than a little surprised to be greeted so on top of the moors. They sat down on the heather and the farmer unfurled a cloth, and the two of them breakfasted on bread, cheese and milk, as the sun arose and warmed the earth.

After all was eaten, Matthew pulled out his pipe and smoked it, and Miles pressed at the bellows under his arm and began to softly singing,

> A shepherd sat him under a thorn
> He pulled out his pipe and began for to play,
> It was on a midsummer day in the morn
> For honour of that holiday.
> A ditty he did chant along
> That goes to the tune of Cater Bordee
> And this was the burden of his song
> If thou will pipe, lad, I will dance for thee.

So pleasant was this interlude that the farmer almost forgot why he had sought out the piper that morning.

"Miles," he began "I have finally thought of a way to keep my wife from working into the Sabbath! This will cure her for certain and it will require your help and assistance."

The men leaned toward each other and Matthew spoke soft and low, punctuated by Mile's occasional nod and the odd outburst of laughter. Soon they stood up, shook hands again and went off the farm. Matthew's wife was not there when they arrived, for she was doing her weekly shopping at Falstone which was as well, for the plan could not work if she had been at home.

That night, which was Saturday, the usual tale began to unfold. The farmer's wife busied herself about the place and Matthew prepared to go to bed.

"Well, wife," he said "Are you coming to bed yet?"

"I'll not be long now," she replied. "Just a few things to do then I'll be finished. You go off and I'll join you soon."

Matthew stopped at the door and said, "Now you won't be working into the Sabbath will you?"

"My! No, of course not," she replied, not daring to look straight at her husband.

"One of these times," continued Matthew, "The devil will hear you and that will be that!" He said this last bit very dramatically as he turned the corner of the stairway, but once out of sight he couldn't help but chuckle to himself, just a little. His wife worked on, doing this, doing that, then redoing them both. The time slipped by and still she continued to work. Eventually, the hands of the clock on the mantle piece pointed straight up, and the mechanism inside began to whirr and click. The melodic chimes sounded out midnight, and as the last note faded away, the wife was startled from her cleaning by a weird and eerie noise.

Somewhere below her, in the depths of the house, there was the terrible wailing of lost souls and tortured voices crying out in pitiful and hideous cries. The screeching grew louder and louder until it seemed to fill the room. The woman dropped the duster that she was holding and began to scream.

Within seconds, Matthew was with her, holding her hand and looking as frightened as she already was.

"Oh Matthew: It's the devil himself. You were right, he's come for me!" she cried as she hid her face in her husband's nightshirt.

"I'll get the Bible!" he said. "You'll have to swear on oath to save yourself!" So saying he took the Bible from the shelf and held it aloft, and in a loud voice said;

> "If my wife this oath give,
> Ne'er to work while she do live
> On another Sabbath Day
> Devil, wilt thou go away?"

... and a clear, distant voice replied:

> "If your wife will keep her trust
> Leave this house and fly I must.
> If her promise be not true,
> I'll come again and claim my due."

Just as soon as the voice finished speaking the wife grasped the book and swore never again to work on a Sabbath and her husband carried her upstairs and put her into bed where she cried herself to sleep after her ordeal.

A little while later, down in the dark kitchen, the door of the cellar was quietly opened, and, from the blackness below, the strange figure of Miles the piper emerged, and with him was his set of Scot's pipes, providers of the sounds from hell. He giggled and quietly lifted the latch on the door and left. The farmer upstairs slept with arm around his wife and a grin all over his face.

Wrap up, rowl up, rowl up thee feetie on it
Wrap up, rowl up, rowl up thee feetie on it
We nivver knew we had a bairnie
Till we heard the greetin' on it

Red-lipped, rosy cheeked, just like the mother of it
Black-haired, knock-kneed, just like the fatha of it
We nivver knew we had a bairnie
Till we heard the greetin' on it

The Easington Hare

Hare coursing was once a very popular practice in rural England. Common men who could not afford the luxuries of riding to hounds or shooting upland game and waterfowl would hunt either with terriers for rabbits or they would course hares. Coursing means that two dogs are set after a hare, and the dog to catch it is the winner. Mostly the hares would escape, unless the men had blocked the gaps in the field, but that was a practice that was frowned upon as unfair.

The men of Castle Eden, in County Durham, were ardent followers of the coursing. Those that possessed greyhounds were rightly proud of them, and every care was taken to keep them fit and happy. One year, the coursing season was quite unlike any other the men had ever experienced. A very large, strange hare had turned up which the dogs were unable to catch, or even keep up with it. It was not the usual dun colour of the local hare population, but was much darker and lacked the red tinge in its coat. It was also a good deal bigger than the others, and seemed to be a whole lot smarter. This new hare would purposely run right under the noses of the dogs to attract their attention, and to get them angry, then when they gave chase it would run straight at the stone walls that surrounded the fields, turning to one side at the last moment. The great lumbering dogs were left no time to turn aside, and their momentum crashed them into the hard stones, knocking them senseless, if they were lucky, and some that were not even died.

The men decided that something would have to be done about this strange creature. They decide to ask one of the farmers, who owned a gun, to come and shoot the hare. The farmer agreed, and said he would shoot the troublemaker so long as he got to keep it to make a stew. To this they agreed, and the farmer followed them to the pasture where the hare kept appearing. They coursed one ordinary hare before the strange one turned up, but eventually there it was, bold as brass, sitting up on its haunches and glaring right at them. The farmer smiled.

"This is going to be too easy," he said. Bang! went the gun, but the hare was still there. The farmer was very surprised, he had not missed a shot since he was a lad. He lifted the gun again and bang! ... he emptied the second barrel. The hare sat defiantly in the same position as before. They could not believe their eyes. Even those who had thought the farmer had aimed poorly on the first shot realised that there was more to this hare than met the eye. Some of the men said simply that they would not course their dogs again. Others said they would find new ground, elsewhere, far from Castle Eden, where they could pursue their sport without having their dogs maimed or killed.

"This is no ordinary hare that we have here," said one of the men. "And I don't think it will go away if we move somewhere else. I think it will follow us." The others thought for a moment, then they agreed with him.

"May I make a suggestion then? We can't catch the thing and it can't even be shot."

"What can we do to get rid of it, then?" asked another of the dog owners. The one who had spoken first suggested that they visit the old man who lived on his allotment at the end of the village, for it was well known that what this old man did not know about animals was not worth knowing. So the men went as one to the gardens to seek the expert's advice. The old chap listened quietly to the younger men as they told the tale of the strange hare that was plaguing their sport. He scratched his head when they were finished, and were they glared at him expectantly.

"I'll tell you," he began. "I've no notion of what might make a hare act in such a manner, if indeed it is a hare. But I can tell you how you can catch it." The men were all pleased to hear this. They could think of no way to trap the hare and this was exactly what they had wanted the

115

old man to came up with. Their spirits were subdued, however, when he suggested that they take his old black hound with them when they next went coursing. Nobody said anything to him though, and one of them took the rope from the old fellow and hauled the great old dog off down the street.

"This thing couldn't catch cold," he said, once out of earshot, and the others agreed. The man who had first suggested the visit to the old man rolled his eyes.

"Well, it's all we've got! Everything else has failed so we may as well give it a try. Perhaps the old man knows something we don't." This was indeed the case, for what the men had failed to notice was that this was a scent hound, and it was not supposed to chase the hare at great speed, but could follow its trail to where it lived. When they reached the field, the hare was already there, watching out for them. They loosed the dog and it lumbered off toward the hare. The hare looked at the dog and the men thought that it might be laughing at them, for surely they did not expect this old thing to catch it? Sure enough, even before the dog had gone half way over the field, the hare ran off in a wide circle, and as though to add an insult to injury, it jumped over the dog's back before making its way off to Castle Eden dene.

"Well, that's that!" said one of the men.

"Wait!" said another. "The dog's following!" At last they realised that the dog could indeed catch the hare, even if it was not very fast about it. Eagerly they followed the black hound as it traipsed its way across the fields and through the copses, flushing the hare time and again, until at last, the hare took off in a straight line, heading for the village of Easington. It was tired and ran very much more slowly than it had earlier, and now the old dog was in pursuit. When it reached the pit village, the hare ran across the green, with the dog right on its tail, and as it made a final bolt for a hole in the bottom of a cottage door, the hound managed to take a bite out of its hind leg!

The men were not far behind and they saw where the hare had gone into the cottage, so when they arrived, puffing and blowing, they banged on the door and called out to be let in. No one answered. They tried the latch. It was locked. So one of the men, a great burly fellow, threw himself at the door and it flew open. There inside the cottage they saw an old woman, sitting in front of the fire and frantically wrapping a bandage around her ankle, which bled quite badly. They realised that it must be she who had turned herself into a hare, and that she must be a witch. They also noticed the tears rolling down her cheeks, and they felt sure that now she had been found out, she would no longer practice her black magic on the folks of Easington and Castle Eden. So they quietly closed the door behind them and said no more about the 'Easington Hare.'

Callaly Castle

The Lord of Callaly had decided to build a new castle and was busy discussing various plans and layouts with some of the local stonemasons and master builders, arguing about costs and so forth. His wife, however, was not overly concerned with how that castle looked, so long it would not be built upon a hill. She preferred the warm, sunny denes and valleys to cold and windy hilltops. But the lord was equally determined to have the structure built at a high vantage point and instructed the builders to lay the foundations on a high fell.

Their arguments were often very heated and seemingly endless.

"If you have your way, we will be stuck down in the bowels of the earth like moles, and I should have no chance to defend myself should we be attacked by an enemy," he said.

"Why do you persist in thinking that someone is bent on destroying the place? There has been peace for years now, and I really don't see why I should be forced to live perched up in the freezing cold clouds where I cannot even smell the sweet flowers of the valley!" she replied. As you may see, they were both prone to exaggerate when trying to produce the better case. So bad were these arguments, that they became the talk of the countryside, and the gossip mongers made even more of them than they already were.

Eventually, when the lord of the castle heard that this difference of opinion was becoming a source of merriment to for miles around, he resolved to put an end to it. Calling his wife into their private chambers, he reminded her of her vows of obedience, and forbade her to argue further, and instructed the men to continue with the new castle in the place that he had chosen. She said nothing, but it was obvious to him that she was very angry. What he did not know was that she resolved to have her way despite his decree.

The construction work began that very same day. Men were everywhere and the land was littered with carts and wheelbarrows and all manner of timber and huge, newly hewn stones. They toiled from sunrise to sunset, ceaselessly digging and carrying until, by the end of the first week, the foundations were complete. And then strange things began to happen on the site. Nothing was ever the same when the workmen arrived in the mornings as they had left it on the previous night. The walls built during the day were torn down and the stones were strewn about the place.

"This is the work of some insane fool who is of the same frame of mind as the mistress," thought the mason. "Tonight I shall hide here and put paid to that little game!" So that night, after supper, the master-builder returned to the site and waited the return of the destructive vandal. But what he saw that night was something that he had neither expected nor bargained for.

After a short wait, the builder could hear a shuffling noise at the other end of the site, where there were still many thorns and briars, and smiling to himself, he leapt out to apprehend the villain. To his enormous surprise there stood before him a huge, furry creature with its arms outstretched ... and in a terrifying voice, it began to wail.

"Callaly Castle built upon a height,
Up in the day, down in the night!
Build it down in Shepherd's Shaw
And it will stand for ever more!"

The builder, his eyes wide with fear, ran off at once and told his tale to the lord, who viewed it with some disbelief.

"Tonight," he said, "I shall come with you to make sure you did not dream this whole thing!" The lord had a suspicion that the craftsman may have been drinking too much ale the night before, for he was known to do so on occasion! Later that evening, when all was still and the stars were bright in the clear sky, the two men were in position. The mason did not like it at all, as he had now convinced himself that it was the devil himself that he had seen on the previous night, but he was assured by his companion that all would be well.

Sure enough, out from the bushes came the low grunts and scraping of the creature as it began to tear down the new walls. Up jumped the lord and up jumped the builder. They began to run toward the creature, but before they had gone more than three steps, it turned to face them, and began its terrible wailing once again.

"Callaly Castle built upon a height,
Up in the day, down in the night!
Build it down in Shepherd's Shaw
And it will stand for ever more!"

The beast stood up to its full height and roared at the top of its lungs and the two men ran fled across the fields, absolutely terrified!

When the next day arrived, the lord of Callaly sent for his wife.

"I have been thinking about your idea of building my new castle on the valley floor," he said. "And I find that it is not so bad after all. How do you like the sound of Shepherd's Shaw?" The wife was of course delighted, but she managed to contain her joy and to look only a little surprised. Then she leaned over and kissed him.

"You know," she said sweetly. "I think if I had chosen the place myself, I would have chosen that very spot!" Then she left the room with her husband not suspecting a thing. Later that day, she handed over the reward she had promised to her servant, who had dressed as the creature in an old sheepskin coat that they had ripped to shreds!

Tis certain that the Dun Cow's milk
Keeps all the Prebends' wives in silk
But this indeed is plain to me
The Dun Cow's self is a shame to see

Hobthrush of Elsdon

There was once a woman who lived in a house called 'The Moat' at Elsdon in Northumberland. She was a very hard-working woman, but somehow she could never bring her housework to an end before she went to bed. She almost always managed to get the big things done, scrubbing worktops and washing, but the once-a-week jobs she would put off until later. Her husband never took food to work with him. Instead, he would come home and eat with his wife. She did not mind this, but it meant that she had to stop her housework and cook his meal. Then, of course, she had to wash up when he had gone, and tidy up the kitchen, so that by the time everything was once again shipshape, it was almost time to make a start on the evening meal.

One morning, she came downstairs and looked through the window at the end of the hallway to see what kind of a day it was. There was glorious sunshine even at that hour.

"Oh, What a lovely day," she said as she stretched her arms and breathed in a long deep breath of fresh morning air. "It's a pity I shall not be able to go out and enjoy it."

She crossed the hall and opened the door that led into the kitchen, and to her surprise she saw that all the jobs she had been unable to finish the night before were complete. A fire was dancing in the grate, the hearth had been polished for the first time in months, and as she gazed through the clean and sparkling windows, she saw the washing was on the line, flapping madly in the breeze.

"My goodness!" she cried as she held up her hands in delighted amazement. She thought at first that her husband had been up all night working hard to achieve all this, but when she went back upstairs and gentle woke him, he denied all knowledge of it. He was equally surprised when he went downstairs and saw how clean and tidy the house was.

"Why this can only be the work of some faerie," he said to his smiling spouse. "They must have heard how hard you work and did this as some kind of reward."

"Well then," she said. "Bless them for it, I feel like a new woman now that I don't have all those chores to worry about." Indeed, she really did seem like a new person, too. She sang as she scrubbed the pots and pans in the sink that day, and whistled back to the thrush that trilled and warbled to her from the apple tree in the garden. She did not work any less hard than she had ever done, nonetheless. All the usual housework still needed to be done, for as they say, 'a woman's work is never done'. On that day, however, the evening meal was a bit special, and at the end of the day, only the dishes soaking in the sink were left for the morning, as all else was complete.

The following day, still in a cheerful mood, the woman went into the kitchen and lo and behold the dishes were washed, dried and back in their cupboard, neat as you please.

"It seems as though my little helper is going to stay," she thought to herself. Each day she worked hard as ever, and tried to get everything finished before bedtime, but as always, she never quite did. There were one or two little things she had to leave for the morrow, and the next day they were always done. So she got into the habit, over the following weeks of leaving out a small gift for her friend, whom she had called 'Hobthrush'. Sometimes, she would leave buttered stottie cake and milk, and when he had been especially helpful, she would leave out blackberry pie and elderberry wine. Always he accepted these gifts, and this pleased her greatly. She often wondered what little Hobthrush looked like—just an average brownie, she expected, not that she'd ever seen one herself but she guessed he would be the same as the descriptions she'd heard from others that supposedly had seen faeries. Nevertheless, she respected the fact that he only ever came in the dark, so that none might see him.

One night, later in the year, he was seen however. The woman's husband had to work late and did not arrive home until well past midnight. As he removed his boots in the hallway, he noticed a faint light shining from the gap under the kitchen door. Quietly, he crept across the hall in his stocking feet and peeped in. There was Hobthrush, scrubbing and polishing for all he was worth. The man watched closely for a while, then silently he took himself off to bed.

The next day the kitchen was once again its usual gleaming self, and there was boiling water to make tea. The husband sat on his chair at the table and spoke quietly.

"I saw your little friend last night."

"Who's that then?" she asked, thinking that he meant someone from the village, or else some neighbour.

"Hobthrush," he told her. Her eyes lit up and she began to ask all manner of questions. She wanted to know what he looked like, what colour his eyes were, how tall he was, how old, The man answered as best he could, which was quite well as he had been careful to note these things in case his wife did ask about them.

"The most remarkable thing about him," said the man, "Is that he is a very raggedy little fellow. He has no shoes, and the shirt and trousers he has are quite threadbare and full of holes."

"Well," replied the wife. "I shall make him up a new set of clothes so that he will be the envy of all his friends!" With that she went to a drawer in the sideboard and produced a pencil and some paper, and instructed her husband to draw the little fellow as best he could. She then began to gather up all the spare materials from her sewing basket. All that day she did nothing at all, but sewed and sewed until at last the suit was finished. And what a splendid suit it was: The coat and trousers were emerald with a fine black belt in the middle. The shoes were made of soft leather, and she had stitched a feather to the hat of scarlet felt. When the suit was finished, she put it on the table, with a small glass of wine and a piece of seed cake, then went to bed feeling very pleased with herself.

The next day dawned and the woman could hardly wait to go downstairs to the kitchen. She burst through the door to see if the suit was still there. It was gone! Hobthrush had accepted her present and had taken the clothes. But what was this? He had not eaten the cake nor drank the wine, and the dishes that she had left in the sink were still there unwashed. It seemed as if the brownie had not done anything except take the suit.

"Oh, well," said the woman to her husband, "He probably rushed off to show his new clothes to his friends, and forgot the cake and wine. He will be back tonight I'm sure."

But Hobthrush never came back that night, nor any other night, for to give a brownie a gift made of anything that will not perish means to set it free and that he will never ever return to that house. So, by her kindness, the woman had unwittingly banished Hobthrush from the Moat, and he has never been seen since.

Trimdon Troughlegs stands on a hill
Poor little Fishburn stands stock still
Butterwick walls are like to fall
Sedgefield is the flower of them all

The Tailor of Cresswell

Cresswell in Northumberland had at one time a very great tailor living in its midst. The unfortunate thing was that this tailor knew he was good, and every time he drank too much, which was almost every time he drank at all, he would corner some poor soul and go on forever about how great he was! Everyone at the local tavern had learned to avoid him when he was drunk, but now and again an unwary traveller or visitor from another village would come into the tavern and the tailor would have a field day. Some men had even stopped going to the pub at all. And some would go only if they knew for sure that the tailor was not going to be there.

One dreary wet night in November, the pub was filled to capacity to celebrate the anniversary of the gunpowder plot, and the tailor was drunk, as usual. He tried to hold conversation with anyone who would listen, but so incoherent was his speech that even those that listened could hardly understand him. This only made him worse, for if he thought no one was listening to him, he often became quite violent and had been known to lash out with his fists. He became very obnoxious and insulting, and as the hours passed by, he decided that he would tell the whole place just how lucky they were to have such a good tailor: He stood up on a chair in the middle of the tavern and began to spout off.

"You people don't realise how well off you are to have someone as great as me living here: There isn't another tailor twixt Tees and Tweed that can turn out a suit as fine as I can. Who thinks there is, hey?" No one was foolish enough to reply. Then he carried on.

"In fact, there's a good chance that I just may be the best in the kingdom, never mind just the North: I could outfit Old Nick himself." And he shook with laughter at his little joke, all the time looking around to see if anyone would try to find fault with his claim. In the chimney corner, wearing a three-corner hat and saying nothing at all to anyone, sat a stranger. The tailor picked him out.

"Hey, you! Did you say something? Are you saying I'm a liar? Well, I've got a few things I would like to tell you!" And the tailor began to roll up his sleeves as though he were about to pick a fight with the stranger. Now, as he crossed the room, he tripped and fell, almost knocking himself unconscious. A great howl went around the room as the others realised that the fool had fallen down, drunk. As they laughingly threw cold water in his face to revive him, the stranger in the corner slipped quietly out of the door. The tailor was slowly beginning to open his eyes and realise what had happened. Of course he had to try to save face and so he pretended that someone had tripped him and, noticing that the stranger had gone, he said in a loud voice:

"See! The cowardly blackguard has sloped off. He knew better than to make a liar of the best tailor in the whole world!" By this time, the long-suffering landlord had had enough, and grabbing him by the scruff of the neck and the seat of the pants, he flung the drunken tailor into the street, and told him not to return until he was stone sober. The tailor was very humiliated at this and was very angry to hear the loud laughter pouring from the pub. He dusted himself off, and began to make his way down the lane that led to his house. Still drunk, he staggered from side to side, and, plunging his hands into his pockets, he stared at the ground and began to sing as he stumbled his way home.

Before very long he stopped dead in his tracks. Directly in front of him was another pair of feet. He slowly raised his eyes from the ground, and there in front of him stood the stranger from the pub. The tailor felt afraid, for though he had sounded brave enough among the others, he was not so willing to fight now that he was all alone. He looked at the stranger who blocked his way. The man's face was shrouded in black but his eyes shone red from beneath the hooded cloak that he wore. He pointed at the tailor, and said in a wiry, thin voice,

"You ... the best tailor between Tees and Tweed! You say you can even rig out the devil. Do you still say so?" The tailor did not wish to appear too much of a coward, and so he replied,

"Yes, I do. What's that to you? Who are you?" Then the stranger threw back the hood of his cloak, and there stood the unmistakable figure of the devil himself. He glared at the quaking man who was by then grovelling on the road before him, shaken and scared.

"I'm your man," said the devil, and, towering over the tailor, he went on. "I require from you, Oh great and mighty tailor, a new suit, ready by this same day next week. And I warn you, if it not perfect as you say it will be, then you will accompany me back to the bowels of the earth, where I will find you work of a different nature!" The poor man became instantly sober and, producing his tape measure, began to size up the devil, though he did so merely for show, as he had no idea of the measurements that he took. The devil raised his arm and vanished, leaving only the smouldering earth on which he stood to bear witness to the whole affair. After a few minutes, the tailor stood up and made his way back to the tavern. When he entered, the men inside realised from the terrified look on his face that there was something wrong, though they had no idea what had troubled him.

When they heard the tailor's story, his neighbours walked him home, and though his wife told him not to be too worried, he slept not one wink that night. The next day, he realised it was a mistake to ever make a bargain with the devil. The only way out was to make sure that there was not a fault to be found in the suit.

"Oh, dear," said the tailor. "The devil will find fault no matter how well I make the suit." But by and by a plan came to him and he thought he might just be able to get himself out of trouble.

One week later, as the pale moon rose over the horizon and lit the lane that led to and from the tavern, it shone also on the tailor, who stood, suit in hand, awaiting the appearance of the devil. He had not long to wait. With a clap of thunder and a flash of lightening, the devil stood before the tailor straight faced and deadly serious.

"Well, master tailor, the best in the whole world," he said sarcastically. "Where is the suit that I charged you to make?" The tailor stepped forward, quite confidently, and handed over the suit. The devil tried it on.

"My, look at this sleeve, it's dangling off the end of my arm!" he said.

"Yes," replied the tailor, "I thought it might, so I made the other a bit shorter." And the devil looked at it and realising that he could not complain by reason of being cheated on length, searched for other faults.

"Why, this pocket is too small by far!" he said.

"Then I'm sure you'll find the other to your liking, sir," replied the tailor. Sure enough, the other pocket was sufficiently oversize to satisfy the keenest of poachers.

"This tail," said the devil. "It is so long that I'm treading on it!" To which the tailor simply replied,

"Then I'm sure the other will admirably suit." The other was, of course, much too short. So the two went on in this manner until they had discussed the entire suit, and the devil realised that no matter where he found fault, the tailor somehow had managed to include some counter-fault to cancel it out. At last the devil reached in his pocket and a handful of coins at the tailor's feet. Then, casting one last evil sneer at him, the devil again vanished and the tailor sighed with relief. He left the coins exactly where they had fallen, and that tailor was never again heard to brag of his work, nor was he ever again seen anywhere near the tavern of that, or any other place.

March wind
Kindles the adder and
Blooms the whin

Nellie the Knocker

Haltwhistle is a town that lies just south of the Roman Wall and near there, once, there was a farm that had a great rock in one of its pastures. This huge stone outcrop had been there since before anyone could recall, and along with it, there had always been the melancholy spectacle of a ghost whom the locals used to call 'Nellie the Knocker.' She got this name from the habit she had of tapping on the rock with a pebble, and making a noise something like that which a thrush makes when it raps a snail shell on a stone. It seemed that she was harmless enough, and after a while she became a part of the everyday scene, and no one paid her very much attention.

The old farmer that owned the farm had grown too long in the tooth to be able to run his farm efficiently, so he sold up and moved into a cottage overlooking the Tyne valley, and was very happy. A younger man bought the farm, and soon this man moved in with his wife and his two sons. The boys were delighted to be in a new place, they were farmers born and bred and they spent every spare minute exploring the farm. They saw the rock of course, and climbed upon it, though the ghost was not there, then they gave it no more thought and went elsewhere to continue the inspection. On the way home, however, they were very surprised, and more than a little scared to see Nellie tap, tap, tapping away at the rock, and without further delay they made for the farmhouse. Their father knew about the ghost for he had even seen her when he surveyed the land, and he explained to the boys that she was harmless and that they should leave her well alone.

His sons, though, just had to know more about poor Nellie. In the evenings they would sit at the side of the field and watch her. They found that if they went too close, she would simply disappear. Night after night she knocked on the rock, and the boys were perplexed to understand why.

"Maybe she's really a blackbird in disguise?" said one.

"Perhaps she's trying to attract someone's attention?" said the other. Neither could think of a reasonable explanation, until at long last, the older of the brothers snapped his fingers,

"I've got it!" he said. "She's trying to break open the rock!" This sounded perfectly plausible to both of them and they agreed that it must be the correct explanation.

Then they wondered what was under the rock, and decided that there simply must be hidden treasure.

The next morning, as they sat at the breakfast table after milking, they begged their father to let them move the stone and look. He was not very keen to have them interfere with the ghost, for as he pointed out, she was not evil in the slightest, and he didn't want to upset her.

"But, Father," interrupted one of his sons. "She always looks so sad, I think she would like us to move the rock for her!" The father was still not convinced, but then one of the boys pointed out that with the great rock removed, he would be able to plough the field and plant it with corn. This certainly appealed to him, and he gave them his permission to try.

The two boys had given little or no thought to the task they were so keen to perform, but now it cam home to them that moving this great rock was not going to be easy at all. They pushed it, they pulled it, they tried to lever it with planks of wood, they even had at it with great sledgehammers, but to no avail. The boulder stood as grand as it ever had. Even when they teamed up the shire horses they could not budge it. They sat and thought long and hard, and eventually one said:

"What we need is some gunpowder or explosives to shift that thing!" Then the other brother smiled.

"I know the very place to get it!" It was mid-morning and the men were working in the quarry a few miles distant, so they got a letter from their father explaining what they wished to achieve. Before the afternoon was an hour old they had returned with enough explosive to move a rock of great size. They packed the explosive around the base of the rock, and dug holes underneath and packed these too, then they lit the fuse and ran as fast as the wind across the field and dived headlong into a drainage ditch.

Just in the nick of time!. As they held their hands over their ears, there came an almighty 'BOOM!' .... and when their ears stopped ringing they ran out and over to where the stone used to be. The earth and splinters of rock were still falling from the sky, and, lo and behold, mixed in with it were thousands of golden coins! The boys stared into the pit left behind by the boulder, and to their delight it too was filled with shining treasure. They were delighted and danced about the field until they could dance no more.

So the family became rich, and prospered for many year after, but no one ever again saw the sorrowful figure of Nellie, a-tap, tap, tapping on that great old rock.

The Henhole

Long ago, the men of the towns and villages of the Cheviots Hills were very keen to hunt the fox, and this is a story of one such outing.

The Cheviots, of course, are sheep country, and all who lived there were no friends of foxes. They rejoiced at the death of every one, for they sometimes made off with a stray lamb. The shepherds and farmers of the village of Kirknewton had a pack of foxhounds and they led them to hunt each weekend of the cold winter. Many who lived thereabouts had saved since they were young to buy a horse or a pony to join in the chase, so it really was a special event. There was one old fellow who had been riding with the hunt for longer than any could remember. His old mare, some joked, was older than he, and was so slow that he rarely caught a glimpse of the fox, for the others always left them so far behind. The old shepherd and his mare became the local joke, and the disrespectful boys of the village would taunt them in the street before the hunt set off.

Now, the shepherd always had hopes that one day, the fox would outwit the faster huntsmen and double back, so that he would have the chance to shout the 'view halloo!' and the others would have to eat their words. This was the only thing that kept up his spirits on those cold winter days.

On one particular day, the hunt set off, and, as usual, the poor little fell pony soon began to lag behind. It found it very difficult to catch its breath in the damp air, and its rider was too kind-hearted to ever think of showing him the whip. So they were content to plod along at their own pace, and to enjoy the sharp embrace of the frosty morning.

Somewhere, up ahead and way out of sight, came the sound of a horn—they had spotted the fox. On and on they charged, over hill and dale, the fox ran through the thickest woods that he could find, but still he was pursued. He ran over stream, and though this threw the dogs for a while, they would pick up his scent fairly quickly, and the hunt was on again. The dogs drew close and the fox could hear them breathing not far behind, their excited howls and baying sent a shiver up his spine, and he knew that if he were caught he would be torn to pieces. But all was not over, for the fox was heading for the Henhole. The Henhole is deep ravine that falls sharply and suddenly from the edge of the fell. The ground was slippery on that day, as the rain had fallen steadily throughout the autumn and now the frost had iced the rim so that it was even more treacherous than usual. There was no bottom in sight and, with the hunt in full flight just a few hundred paces behind, the sly fox side-stepped the edge and sat motionless in a depression to one side.

Now, though you may expect that the huntsmen went tumbling over the brink of the Henhole, they were not so silly as the fox had hoped, and as they came to the lip of the ravine, they pulled up their horses and peered down. One of them said,

"Well, we can't be expected to go any farther, this is the Henhole, and we all know that it is full of strange faerie folk who won't take kindly to our trespassing"

The others agreed, for it was well known in those days that the faeries that lived in the Henhole often lured unsuspecting travellers down there, and they were not seen again. So they were about to give up the chase, when, from somewhere deep in the mists below, they heard the enchanting sounds of voices sing to them. The song seemed be telling them to come down into the Henhole, and that all would be well, and the men and the dogs, and even the fox, were lured over the edge by the voices of the spirits of the hills. One by one they dismounted and went down the steep slope, into the mist that swirled and hid the singers from view. Soon every one of the hunters was gone. All, that is, but one.

Long after the last of them had disappeared, up the hill came the plodding fell pony with the old shepherd upon its back. By the time he reached the edge of the Henhole, the song the others heard had stopped, and he was not enchanted. He saw the track of the men and horses going over the cliff, and knew what had lulled them to go into the Henhole. Sadly, he turned his old steed around and trundled off home, aware that only the slowness of his old nag had saved him from the fate that his fellows had met only a few minutes earlier.

When Cheviot you see put on his cap
Of rain we'll have a wee bit drap

The Consett Giants

Normally, giants cannot abide each other's company, but there were once three giants who lived together all their lives. That was because they were all brothers. They were Ben, Cor and Con, and they lived on the hills where the Tyne, the Wear and the Tees rivers all rise.

These brothers were never far away from one another, and they were very happy in their lives, so they never had cause to grow bitter and mean, and they never ever hated the men of the valleys. They kept themselves to themselves, high up on the moors, or in the dale heads. They were extremely strong, and kept their muscles in tone by forging iron into great wheels, or plough shares, and this they achieved with the use of an enormous hammer which had been given to them long ago when they were only young lads. The hammer was enchanted, and was made of a faerie metal that never wore out, but there was one drawback to it.

A spell had been cast over the magical hammer, and the giants were obliged to pass it from one to another, as they had but one. They were sometimes a long way away from whoever had it, which meant it had to be thrown a great distance. The spell stated that should the hammer ever be dropped, then all three brothers would vanish from the face of the earth. Now this may have made some people shy about ever using such a tool, but to the giants it was nothing, for they were very strong, and they had the keenest eyesight. Whenever one of them wished to use it, he would whistle loudly, and the next moment the air would be filled with a high pitched swoosh as the hammer hurtled across the hills. No one ever missed it, and soon it became so easy that they were able to catch it without even looking up from what they were doing.

As the years went by, the giants never looked any older, and none of them felt the passage of time, until one day, Con stood up to stretch his legs. He noticed that he could not see the village of Lanchester, even though he was only standing over by Wittonstall, which is no distance to a giant. He knitted his eyes and tried again, this time he could just make out the smoke as it curled up out of the cottage chimneys.

"That's better," he thought. "For a moment I thought I was getting a little short sighted. Must be very misty between here and Lanchester." All the same, he did not mention this to his brothers, for the consequences were grave indeed. He thought that if they suspected he was losing his eyesight and might drop the hammer—and that meant the end of them all—they would leave him behind, and he could not bear that. So from then on, he began to work closer to the others so that the hammer did not have so far to travel.

This seemed to be a perfectly satisfactory solution, and neither of his brothers noticed as, day by day, he was actually getting closer and closer to them. Even so, he called for the hammer less and less.

One morning, in the summer when the sun was up before anything else, and its light bathed the moors and fells, the giants were working away. Ben was at Lanchester, Cor at Whittenstall, and Con about halfway between. Con, without a second thought, gave out a shrill whistle and held his am aloft in anticipation. He heard the hammer being thrown, but to his dismay, his sight failed completely at that very moment. In desperation he leapt toward the sound of the flying hammer, and even managed to touch the shaft as it whistled by, but he had missed it, and the three giant brothers vanished in an instant, never to be seen again.

There is one reminder that these giants roamed those dales, for you may still see the depression that the hammer left in the ground where if fell, and that's where the town got its name: Consett.

Sir John Duck

John Duck arrived one day in the city of Durham penniless and seeking his fortune. He was a butcher, and thought that such an honourable trade would keep him fed no matter where he went. But the butchers of Durham were all freemasons and were not prepared to employ him in any of their shops, especially since all of them were hard pushed to pay their own apprentices. Time after time he asked the butchers to let him show them how skilful he was but time and again they turned him down until, in the end, John Duck left the city unable to afford even the humblest lodgings anymore.

He had decided to walk and try again in the larger towns in the east of the county, though he was desperately poor, and was not at all sure he would be able to walk that far without having eaten for several days. He stopped at a bridge and, dangling his legs over the side, he saw the reflection of a great black bird in the rippling waters of the

River Wear. Looking up, he saw high above him a raven, for ravens were not so rare in those days, and it had something in its beak. Ravens are known for the strange, playful habit that they have of dropping things from their beaks, then catching them before they reach the ground. This one was doing just that. John watched the fascinating bird as it rolled over on its back in mid-air, and then quickly turned and tumbled after the object it had dropped.

"Ah, I wish I was as free as you are," sighed the young man. "Flying up there without any care in the world." This thought made him even more depressed, and his troubles weighed more heavily than ever. He noticed that the raven was still up above him, nearer now than at first, and suddenly, the great black bird dropped the object it was playing with at his feet. It did not seem to be a stick, nor something to eat. John went over to it and discovered that it was a gold coin. He picked it up and turned to thank the raven, but the bird had already flown off. Now he could go back to the city and buy a hot meal, and perhaps a bottle of wine. This one gold piece was like a fortune to him!

He was a very sensible fellow, though, and he thought for a long while about how he should spend the coin. Just then, along the road that led to Sherburn village, there came a farmer driving three cows.

"Where are you going with those cows?" asked John, politely, and the tired looking farmer looked up.

"To Durham, to sell them to the first man that wants them!" He explained that he had driven them for almost ten miles and in that distance they had run off no fewer than six times, so he would be pleased to see the back of them. John asked his price, but it was a little more than the coin was worth.

"How would it be if I gave you this gold coin and drove them the rest of the way myself?" The farmer thought for a moment.

"Very well! You're getting a good deal, but it's worth it to save me the trouble of walking them that extra few miles." The two men slapped each other's palm, as was the custom then, and parted smiling.

John Duck took the cows into Durham and sold them at a handsome profit, more than enough to buy his dinner and pay for new lodgings, and to leave sufficient to wheel and deal again and again. He was a renewed man, and before much longer he became a rich man. He bought land all around the city of Durham, and one day he was elected mayor. Why, he even went on to be knighted, Sir John Duck.

So the penniless lad who had almost quit the city for good became one of its most prominent citizens, and he never forgot the day when providence smiled upon him and, as a lasting tribute, he built a hospice at Lumley to care for those to whom fate had not been so kind.

The Sage's Student

The North Riding once had a wise Sage who was skilled in the ways of sorcery and its application. He spoke and understood every dialect of Britain, as well as dozens of foreign languages. In one room of his house, there was an oak lectern, carved in the image of a raven, whose back served as a book rest. The volume that constantly lay there was full of the mysteries of creation.

Occasionally he would take the key from the gold chain around his waist and unlock the leather bound book and spend hours learning and re-learning its secrets. It told of the heavens and the angels there, of the abyss beneath the earth and of the terrible things that dwelt in the cold waters. It told of dark demons and how to summon them, how to trap and enslave a spirit from beyond. So you can understand why he suffered none but himself to look upon the pages of this book, and kept it locked at all times.

This wizard, it was said, had been on the earth for longer than anyone's grandfather could remember, and as the years were beginning to lie heavily upon his shoulders, he decided, after great consideration, to take in an apprentice, to follow in his footsteps when he had gone.

The choice was arrived at one day when he heard of a boy whose parents had drowned at sea, and had left him all alone in the world. They had been quite well off, and the boy could read and write, and was already very proficient in the use of figures. So the old man took him in and began to teach him the incantations of preparation, which the boy had to repeat, day after day, time after time, until he knew them by heart.

After some months, the boy, who was very bright, asked if he might move on to something a little more exiting. The sage said that he was not yet strong willed enough to control himself, let alone any demon that he might come upon, and he urged the boy to keep up his study, and to learn the virtue of patience. Soon after this conversation took place, the sage was called upon by a local farmer who said his wife was ill with some sickness of the soul, and she had sent her husband to seek him out that he might cure her problem. The sage left in such a great hurry that he forgot to lock the great book, and so when the apprentice entered the room and was astounded to discover that at long last he would be able to read the ancient runes written in the beginning of time. He hurried over to the lectern and, standing on a chair, he looked at the open page. To his dismay, however, he realised that it was written in some antique tongue of which he had no knowledge. There were beautiful pictures, and magnificently embossed capitals, but they meant nothing to him. He tried holding out his arms, and saying things like, 'make gold', and 'food and wine,' but nothing seemed to make the magic work for him.

"Well," thought the boy, "At least I've managed to get a look at the book, I just wish that I could make something magical happen." As he spoke he was unwittingly tracing the outline of the words on the page with his finger. As he reached the tail end of the last figure, the room seemed to grow darker, and he fancied he could hear the sound of something rumbling in the distance, like thunder on the moor. Just then the candle on the table flickered, and the glasses began to ring on the shelves. Suddenly, with an almighty bang, there appeared in the middle of the room, a great, brawny, and extremely ugly creature that smelled like decay and smouldered like pitch. The apprentice had summoned the prince of the devils, Beelzebub.

"Set me your task!" thundered the demon.

The boy was absolutely terrified, and could do no more than blink and tremble in his boots.

"Set me your task!" boomed the demon again, in an even louder voice. The boy remembered then that should the demon ask a third time, and remain unanswered, he would claim the soul of whoever had summoned him. Desperately, he tried to think of something to occupy the devil.

"Set me your ... "

"Water that plant!" cried the boy, pointing to a potted flower on a desk at the side of the room. It was a silly thing to say, but it was all he could think of to save his soul. Beelzebub looked insulted, but an evil smile crept to his lips as he disappeared through the door. For a moment the boy thought he had gone for good, but almost as soon as he had thought it the demon re-appeared carrying a rain barrel, of all things, full to the brim with water, and he poured the whole thing over the plant. The apprentice looked wide-eyed at the mess that resulted. Within seconds the demon returned with another barrel of water that he threw into the room. Then another, and another and on and on, until it seemed that he was passing himself on the way in as he went out. The room was filling up with water, and the poor boy kept screeching.

"Stop, stop!" But to no avail—he did not know how he had summoned the devil in the first place, and he certainly did not know how to get rid of him. Beelzebub laughed louder and louder each time he stepped into the room, alas and alack, the water was now up to the boy's neck, and he knew of no way to escape drowning. Tears began to roll down his face though they were hard to see amongst the water already splashed onto his cheeks.

It was at that moment the sage appeared in the doorway, and stopped dead in his tracks. The old man looked around in dismay and glared at the apprentice ferociously. The boy sat shivering on the table where the plant had formerly stood. The wizard raised his arms high and began to chant a mystical rhyme. The room began to swim before the boy's eyes and he became so dizzy that he fell from the table and banged his head. Everything went black.

When he opened his eyes, all was as it had been before the farmer called. The boy did not understand, for all the furniture was dry, and there was the wizard, reading the great book. A knock upon the door, and on answering it, the apprentice saw it was the farmer, asking the sage to visit his sick wife. This time, however, when the wizard left the house and left the book unlocked, the boy remembered his vivid dream and was wise enough not to look, and instead continued with his own studies.

Sir Guy the Seeker

The darkness of the raging storm made it quite difficult to be sure whether or not it was still day as the young knight battled his way into the headwind. He was on the road North, homeward bound, when he encountered this wild and sudden weather. The icy gale whipped up the sea into an angry cauldron, the great white plumes sending up a fine spray that mingled with the sleet to soak the unfortunate Sir Guy to the very skin. Tightly he wrapped his only protection, a woollen blanket, around his shoulders, and he tried to shelter his head to the leeward side of his horse's neck. Between each successive gust of biting rain, he raised his eyes to search the darkness for a light, for any sign of shelter from the fury of the bitter night. It seemed that it was not to be. Time and again he scanned the countryside, but never a glimmer spied. Then, as a lightening flash lit up the world for a second or two, he saw, a mile or so ahead on the horizon, the silhouette of a castle, black against the grey backdrop of stormy sky.

With his flagging spirits revived at the sight, the knight urged his tired steed toward the castle, and an hour later saw the two of them at the main gate. This was Dunstanburgh Castle, though he did not have any notion of that. Sir Guy was only too pleased to be out of the teeth of the storm, somewhere that he might get food and a fire to curl up in front of, somewhere he might rest for the night. The knight dismounted and boldly approached the door. Grasping the huge doorknocker he beat it hard down onto the strike-plate and the sound rang out even above the rolling thunder. Again and again he knocked, but it seemed that he was not to be answered. Once again he began to despair, for as he looked up to the castle, he could see no light, and it occurred to him that this may be only a ruin, or perhaps deserted for some reason.

At that moment, an unusually close bolt of lightening lit up the porch and there in the doorway stood the outline of a great man, at least eight feet tall. Sir Guy's horse took fright at this spectacle and it reared up and bolted into the night. The giant spoke.

"Come in, Sir Knight."

Sir Guy followed this servant into the castle and they walked through corridors and passages until they were in a great room.

"This is indeed a strange place," the knight said to the giant. "I never saw a man so big as yourself, nor a room which is so bright, yet has not a single torch to light it."

The servant replied by merely pointing to the far end of the hall. Sir Guy strained his eyes to see what the giant might be pointing to. At the end of the hall, there appeared to be people. Yes, there were at least two men seated in throne-like chairs. The knight slowly walked the length of the room, each footfall seeming louder than the last. Neither man looked up. On went the knight until at last he could see that these were kings, and they appeared to be either dead or sleeping. He peered closely at their faces. They looked like waxen images, but very lifelike. Sir Guy decided that he did not like the look of them at all. In the hand of the king who sat to the left, as the knight looked at them, there was a sword. It was the finest he had ever seen, jewel-encrusted and engraved with all manner of exotic birds and animals. The king's hand was open, as though he was offering the blade to the young man. He looked over to the other king, and in his hand was a very splendid hunting horn, ornately carved and inlaid with silver, and trimmed and lipped with pure gold. It was the finest he had ever seen. This king too held it in a manner that seemed to invite the knight to take it.

Sir Guy looked over to the servant, who had stood silently behind him whilst he had examined the twin kings.

"What means this?" asked the knight. Again the reply was a gesture of the hand and the servant pointed to what appeared to be a large mound of ice, which had somehow materialised between them. Sir Guy carefully made his way to the mound and looked at it hard. He could not see through the frosting, but there seemed to be something inside. He leaned over and rubbed the top with his hand. It was not cold, as he had expected. Again he looked and there inside was something that was to change his whole life from that moment on.

Deep within the coffin, for coffin it was, there lay a beautiful girl. She was the finest that he had ever seen. Her eyes were emerald green and her complexion flawless. Her lips seemed to shine with the crimson glow of an autumn sunset. Sir Guy fell instantly in love with this wonderful princess. For the longest time he gazed speechless at the girl. Then he roused at last.

"Why does she not move? She is not dead, for I feel it in my soul."

"No, she lives," replied the servant, "But she exists under a spell, a spell from which, good sir knight, you may release her."

The knight looked anxiously at the giant, and begged to know how he might win the princess from the enchantment under which she lay. This is what the servant told him.

"Long ago, the princess was placed under this spell, and no one has yet broken it. The spell is simple enough, for all you must do is either to sound the horn, and smash the coffin with the sword ... or break the coffin then sound the horn. But be warned ..." The giant looked straight into the knight's eyes, "If you take the wrong one first, you will lose the chance forever. Think carefully before you chose, sir knight!"

Sir Guy was perplexed indeed. Which should he take first? The sword? Or the horn?

He looked from one to the other and then at the beautiful girl lying quite still by his side. Should he sound the horn first, and then break the case? Or was it the other way? The knight was almost beside himself trying to think of a logical answer. Of course, there was none, he must make a simple choice, one or the other.

"Your time is up," said the servant "You must now choose." Sir Guy looked again at the girl.

"There must be witchcraft at work, I am so besotted that my heart hurts," he whispered. With that he turned and stepped over to the kings. For a moment he closed his eyes, then he quickly grabbed the horn and blew out a long high blast.

All became instantly transformed, and the poor knight found himself on the floor of the porch, where his horse had bolted at the sight of the giant servant. Warm sunshine had replaced the cold weather of the storm, and the horse was there by his side once more. Slowly he realised that he must have chosen wrongly! Sir Guy frantically pushed open the door and began to search the castle for the hall in which he had seen his beautiful princess, but alas; he would see her never again. So deep was this wound of love the knight suffered, that he spent the rest of his days wandering around Dunstanburgh

Castle and the immediate area in search of his lost love. But he never did find her, and some say that he still looks for her, and that if you are ever there during a stormy night, you too might see Sir Guy the Seeker, still searching for the beautiful girl whom he loved and lost.

Rothbury for goat milk
Cheviot for mutton
Cheswick for its bread and cheese
Tynemouth for a glutton

The Tide at Morpeth

Long ago, the town of Morpeth in Northumberland was buzzing with the news of the arrival of Michael Scott, the great magician.

"The king of Scotland had sent Michael Scott to France to secure a treaty between the two countries," said the mayor of Morpeth to his councillors. "But because he was dressed shabbily, Michael was not allowed into the palace to speak with the king. This was not what the magician had come all the way to Paris to hear, and he became quite annoyed, and again sent a message inside, this time with the warning that if he was not heard, he would bring the palace down about the ears of all inside.

"He made his horse stamp its feet, and the ground shook mightily, and the palace walls began to shake and spill out plaster dust onto the king and his court below. So Michael Scott had made the king of France do what all the other ambassadors had failed to do!"

There was a reception planned for the magician while he stayed in Morpeth, and during the banquet, he said to the mayor, "You have been very kind to me. Is there anything I can do for you?" So the mayor called together the council and they discussed what favour they might ask. They discussed many things they should have the magician do for them. They could ask for gold, or new houses to live in, or maybe he would give them wealth beyond their dreams!

"No, no!" said the oldest and wisest of them. "We must ask nothing for ourselves, for if he decides that we are a greedy people, he will undoubtedly be very angry, and likely we shall get more than we bargained for!" The others saw the sense in this and they agreed.

"We ought to ask for something for our town, then we shall all gain benefit from it." They sat around their conference table and eventually agreed that what they would like best was that Morpeth become a very prosperous town. The way to do this, they thought, was to have a fine port like the people of Newcastle had, so that they too would receive lots of merchant shipping and foreign trade. There was only one drawback to this idea, and that was that there was no tide at Morpeth, for it lay too far inland, and it mattered not how good a seaport they built, it would be useless if the ships could not reach it. So the mayor and his council decided they would ask the great magician to bring the tide to Morpeth.

Michael was pleased when he found that they did not want him to give them all riches and gold, which is what people usually asked of him, and so he told them that he would do everything within his power to bring this change about. Late that night he called in the men of the council, and told them that he had a spell which would bring the tide up the River Wansbeck, all the way to Morpeth!

"This is a simple plan, but you must be sure to follow it to the letter. If you do not, the spell will break and the opportunity will be lost forever." The men all listened carefully to what Michael said, and what he said was this:

"Choose among you someone who can run fast and far, and have him stand on the seashore at daybreak when the first tide comes to its full height. At that moment he must turn and run toward Morpeth as fast as he can, and on no account must he look back, else the water will rush back to the sea and never return."

The men listened in excitement and talked about it into the small hours of the next day. It was decided that the runner would be the young man who ran each year in the fell races across the Pennines in the Lake District of Cumbria, for he had both speed and stamina, and they felt sure that if anyone could outrun the tide, it was he. The young man was only too pleased to do this for the town in which he had been born, and bright and early the next day he proudly stood on the shore of the North Sea, waiting for the signal to begin his run to Morpeth.

The time arrived and the tide was full, and, amid the encouraging cheers of the people on the beach, the young lad set off. What happened then came as a completed surprise to him, for as he ran, he began to hear the terrible wails and cries of the water spirits as they ran along just behind him. The runner was very frightened by these weird and horrible sounds, and felt an overwhelming desire to look around to see what was making them, but he remembered what the magician had said, and he kept on running. The closer he got to Morpeth, the louder grew the noises behind him, begging, it seemed, for him to turn around and set them free.

Time seemed endless to him, and his legs felt as though they were filled with lead, dragging along, tiring him out step by step. He could feel the icy breath of the faeries on the back of his neck, and their cold little hands as they grabbed at the strands of his hair that flowed out behind him. At last he could stand it no longer, and he threw one quick glance over his shoulder to satisfy his curiosity. No sooner had he done this that the mournful cries turned to hideous laughter, and the spirits of the sea scorned and jaded him for his failed effort to bring the tide away from where it was meant to be. And the water rushed back down the valley to the sea, and has never since returned to Morpeth.

The Witch of Seaton Delaval

One night, long ago, a young man was making his way home along a cart-track that led to Wallsend. The wind was high and he had his cloak wrapped tightly about his shoulders to keep out the bite of the fresh spring air. As he passed a church to his right, he noticed there was a light inside, but he was not overly concerned as people often lit candles at the Lady alter which gave off a dim light such as he had seen. He continued on his way without a second thought. A way farther down the track, however, he met two men cushing cattle from the fields.

"Why are you moving the cows so late in the evening?" he asked.

"Why, it's the last day of April," said one of the men with surprise. "Tomorrow is May Day and if we leave them out in the open tonight they'll be cursed by witches for certain!" Then the traveller remembered that on the last day of April wicked witches gathered and cast spells upon the people and their animals. He had seen the damage that these witches could cause, he had seen the animals struck with disease and the crops fail in the fields for no apparent reason. And just then he remembered the light he's seen in the church and it occurred to him that it might be the black witches meeting before working their mischief.

At once he turned about and ran toward the church where the eerie glow still burned within. He climbed up to a window and peered into the shadowy interior. There, in a circle, around the flickering glow of a black candle, was a coven of black-robed witches. As he stared in disbelief, he could hear the incessant chanting and the voice of a central figure who was standing over a boiling pot. One by one she dropped things into the cauldron and sang:

"This is to cloud their joy and mirth
This is to kill the lambs at birth
This is to spoil the food in shops
And this is to burn and rot their crops!"

This was all too much for the young man, he was by this time very angry and he thought to himself, "Not if I can prevent it!" and saying this he burst through the church door and grabbed the witch next to the cauldron. She kicked and bit him fearfully but he did not release her. The other witches fled in panic, but he did not bother to chase them, satisfied that he had caught the ringleader. Despite the noise and pain she inflicted, he managed to haul her off to the prison where she remained until the day the trial arrived.

By this time, news had spread far and wide, and people came from all around to bear witness against the witch. The people were insistent that it was she who had been responsible for every ill occurrence of the past year. Not surprisingly, she was found guilty and sentenced to be burned at the stake. As the old witch was led away to the burning post, however, and the faggots were piled up around her, the people began to soften, for although she had done them such wrong in the past they felt sorry for her. Someone said:

"Why not grant her a last request?" and others in the crowd agreed it was a good idea. So one of the officials approached the witch and asked if there was anything they might do for her before the sentence was carried out. The old hag looked at him with an evil glint in her eye and said in a soft voice:

"Why, that's very kind of you. I know I have done the good people of Seaton Delaval a great wrong, but I repent with all my heart. All I ask is that you bring me two little wooden plates and set them beneath my feet. Mark you," she added, "They must be brand new and never used before!"

"Why, I have brand new dishes," said one woman in the crowd. "I'll go and get them right away." And she ran off to her house to get them. She reappeared ten minutes later with the two plates. The official set them under the witch's feet and, almost at once, a strange whirring sound filled the air. To everyone's astonishment, the witch flew up into the sky with the wooden plates supporting her. As she passed overhead she cursed the villagers and vowed she would make them pay dearly for trying to burn her. The people were frightened and began to run around in panic. But the woman who had brought the plates cried aloud:

"Do not fear! I had suspected some trickery and I only gave her one new plate. The other has been used a thousand times! Look!" ... and as she spoke the used plate fell away from the witch's foot and she came tumbling out of the sky. Many looked away as she hit the ground, but just as many saw the witch of Seaton Delaval get her just reward.

Berwick-upon-Tweed
Newcastle-upon-Tyne
Alnwick for white bread
Morpeth for swine

~ * * * ~

Printed in Great Britain
by Amazon